A Vow of
Fidelity

A Vow of Fidelity

VERONICA BLACK

St. Martin's Press ⋙ New York

Library of Congress Cataloging-in-Publication Data

Black, Veronica.
A vow of fidelity / by Veronica Black.
p.   cm.
ISBN 0-312-14064-9
1. Joan, Sister (Fictitious character)—Fiction.
2. Women detectives—England—London—Fiction.
3. Nuns—England—London—Fiction.
4. London (England)—Fiction.   I. Title.
PR6052.L335V6833   1996
823'.914—dc20   95-46781   CIP

First published in Great Britain by Robert Hale Limited

First U.S. Edition: March 1996
10 9 8 7 6 5 4 3 2 1

A Vow of
Fidelity

One

Sister Joan of the Order of the Daughters of Compassion sat demurely on the only hardbacked chair in the studio, sipping a bitter lemon, watching others gyrate in the centre of the room, legs flashing, arms windmilling. Faces blurred into the music and one of the dancers, hand outstretched, approached her, laughing into her face with open invitation in the narrow dark eyes. She set her glass down on a side table and rose, the ample skirts of her grey habit flapping above her ankles, her short white veil whipping across her face as she was whirled into the music and the colour.

'I ought not to be here,' she muttered, and pulled away, leaning back, becoming the fulcrum round which the dancers swirled and dipped and bobbed.

Then someone hurled a pot of scarlet paint against the walls and the liquid ran down, staining the whiteness, forming pools on the bare boards, dyeing the feet of the dancers. The music had changed, becoming a loud clacking noise, a voice proclaiming, 'Christ is risen!'

'Thanks be to God!' Sister Joan answered hastily, tumbling from the narrow bed to her knees on the floor with the ease of long practice.

That, she thought, had been a dream and a half! After eight years in the religious life her subconscious mind still threw up the occasional nightmare to pierce her sleep with foreboding. They came less and less often but they still came, unbidden and disturbing.

Five o'clock on a chilly September morning. She rose from her knees, poured cold water from the ewer into the basin, washed face and hands, cleaned her teeth, slipped off her

5

nightdress and cap and drew on the regulation bra, knickers and tights without looking at her small, trim body. Two long slips, one of white cotton, one of grey flannel were covered by the grey habit with its high neck and wide sleeves. She laced up her low-heeled black shoes, tied the white cord girdle about her slim waist, clipped the crucifix and rosary into place at her side, brushed her short, curly black hair and adjusted the short white veil with her fingers moving expertly without the aid of a mirror, and stood up, music and dancing and splashing red paint gone from her brain.

Opening her cell door she joined the line of sisters making their way to the chapel. Hands folded at waist level, blue eyes lowered, she descended the wide polished staircase up which beautifully dressed ladies had once mounted with their escorts to the ballroom above. That ballroom was now divided into refectory and recreation room, but the moulded ceilings with their faint tracery of gold leaves, the slightly curved balustrade with its carved newel post remained. The last of the Tarquin family had gone and high on the Cornish moors a convent stood, holding the memories of more gracious times deep in its stone.

Across the wide hall with its polished parquet floor, turn left into the corridor which bypassed the two tiny parlours with their dividing grille where visitors were welcomed, past the row of narrow, arched windows that ran along the outer wall and into the chapel proper with the sacristy leading off it and a flight of spiral stairs leading from the side of the Lady Altar to the library and storerooms above.

Genuflecting to the High Altar she stepped into her usual place, blessing herself and beginning her silent, private prayers. All about her the others were immersed in their own worship, each head bowed, looking to anyone who might be clinging to the ceiling like two rows of peas in grey pods, except that each one of these women with whom she had lived since coming to the convent three years before was a definite and separate individual, from Sister Perpetua, the infirmarian, with her quiff of grey-ginger hair and blunt manner to delicate Sister Martha who kept the enclosure gardens fruitful, almost singlehanded, and had the energy to lug bags of potatoes and manure around without working up more than the mildest of sweats.

Mother Dorothy rose at the appointed hour to give out the subject for meditation.

'The parable of the buried talents,' she said in her cool, crisp voice, the light from the sanctuary lamp glinting on her steel-framed spectacles.

Sister Joan repressed a grimace. Sometimes she felt a pang of guilt at the thought of all the pictures unpainted, the exhibitions unheld, the money unearned, the fame that might well have become hers, though most of the time she was forced to admit that her talent was a slight one, fame something that happened to other people, and the only way in which she could have earned a living was probably by designing greetings cards.

At 7.30 precisely Father Stephens emerged from the sacristy to offer mass. This was a low-mass, in contrast to the Sunday service. Father Stephens always offered the mass as if he thought the Pope might be watching and marking him down for rapid promotion, Sister Joan thought, and felt her lips twitching into the beginnings of a stifled chuckle. Father Stephens was young, blond and handsome, rather less confident than he appeared to be but with a very proper sense of his own dignity. She preferred Father Malone who was elderly and absentminded and bought his old mother a new hat every Easter, carrying it home to Galway with a loving heart.

The final blessing pronounced and the Angel of the Presence dismissed, Father Stephens withdrew. Mother Dorothy rose.

'There will be a meeting of all the community in the parlour at ten o'clock,' she announced. 'It's of some importance in the life of the community so please be on time.'

Sister Joan filed out again, up the staircase into the refectory. A long oak table with benches down both sides and chairs at head and foot, a reading lectern, a side table from which food was served comprised the only furniture. Slices of dry brown bread, a large bowl of red apples and mugs of coffee were ranged along the table. The Sisters ate standing up, permitted to talk and move around if they wished. Father Malone called it 'gossip time', but the gossip was mild. Padraic Lee had been fined for poaching again.

'Which seems very unfair since we had the benefit of the fish,' Sister Teresa said ruefully.

She had been fully professed after Easter and was now lay

sister, the Martha of the community. With her rosy cheeks and infectious laugh she looked as if she had been born for the role of Martha, Sister Joan thought. She was also an excellent cook.

'We shall of course offer to reimburse Mr Lee for the money he has lost,' Mother Dorothy said.

Sister Joan wondered how she proposed to do that. Each house of the order was supposed to be self-supporting, only the partly enclosed sisters being permitted to work, with the proviso that the employment didn't interfere with their spiritual duties. At the moment money was even tighter than usual. Sister Martha sold some of the produce from the garden in the local market and Sister Katherine sold her exquisite lace, mainly to brides and mothers of babies about to be baptised, and little Sister David worked as a translator when she wasn't cataloguing the books in the library, writing her series of children's booklets on the saints (which hadn't yet found a publisher), and taking care of the chapel, but that was all. I could sell some paintings, Sister Joan mused, and frowned, uneasily aware that she was more interested in expressing herself than in earning money for the convent.

At ten o'clock she entered the shallow antechamber at the left of the front door, tapped on the inner door and entered the prioress's parlour. This was a beautiful room, huge windows looking out over the grass that stretched to the wall dividing the convent grounds from the track that meandered across the moor, past the Romany camp and the old schoolhouse towards the town. The brocade-covered sofas and spindle-legged chairs had long gone, replaced by filing cabinets and a flat-topped desk and a row of stools, but there were still silk panels on the walls and gilt roses at the cornices.

'If you please, Mother, do you require my attendance?' Sister Hilaria, novice mistress, had popped her large face round the door.

'The entire community, Sister,' Mother Dorothy said firmly, 'including your postulant.'

'Come along, Bernadette.' Sister Hilaria fussed her charge forward, looking like a large rabbit with only one of its litter surviving.

Sister Joan glanced towards the pink-smocked figure, the large white bonnet covering the shaven head effectively cutting off the girl's vision at each side. Bernadette was new, the only postulant they had since Sister Marie had moved on into the novitiate proper. It must be lonely for Bernadette, forbidden to receive visitors, allowed to speak only to the prioress, the novice mistress and the priests, and she had almost a full year to go before she could grow her hair one inch and wear the grey habit and black veil of the novice. It was impossible to tell. The lowered head and eyes and folded hands gave nothing away.

'Are we all here?' Mother Dorothy looked round.

'Just one moment, Mother.' Sister Perpetua was settling Sister Mary Concepta who had struggled up from the infirmary where she and Sister Gabrielle spent their nights and most of their days. 'There! Now we're all comfortable again!'

'Speak for yourself, Sister!' Sister Gabrielle said sharply. 'At eighty-six I reserve the right to be uncomfortable! Good morning, Mother. Has the meeting begun?'

'By your leave, Sister.' Mother Dorothy allowed a faint reproof to enter her tone. Oblivious to it, Sister Gabrielle said cheerfully, 'Right then! Let's begin!'

'It is a question of money,' Mother Dorothy said, seating herself at her desk. 'We all know that jobs are very hard to come by and that we are, in any case, limited in the work we can do. Since the local school closed our income has been whittled away month by month, and unfortunately the building needs upkeep. We are not in the least extravagant but a certain amount of expenditure is necessary for survival. I have been thinking about the problem for some time and I have reached a conclusion.'

'Euthanasia,' Sister Gabrielle said darkly.

'I beg your pardon, Sister?' Mother Dorothy stared at her.

'The modern way of dealing with the aged,' Sister Gabrielle elaborated. 'Depend upon it, Mary Concepta, one of these days soon we'll taste a bitterness in our cocoa and then it'll be requiem and two less mouths to feed. Don't look so shattered! I'm joking!'

'Rather tastelessly, Sister dear,' Sister Mary Concepta said.

'May we get on?' Mother Dorothy to whom Sister Gabrielle was sometimes a thorn in the flesh rapped her pencil on the desk. 'As I was saying I have thought deeply about the problem. Apart from Sister Hilaria and myself we are eight sisters, one novice and one postulant – twelve in all. We must become – not prosperous but able to maintain the community without begging or getting into debt. I have been thinking that one way in which we could earn money would be by holding weekend and week-long retreats – quiet holidays for people who need to recharge their batteries so to speak.'

'In the convent?' Sister David sounded uncertain.

'I was thinking of the postulancy,' the Prioress said.

Eleven minds promptly switched to the old dower-house at the back of the abandoned tennis court where novice mistress and postulants lived, largely separate from the main community.

'But where would Sister Hilaria and Sister Bernadette go?' Sister Marie asked.

'I have been thinking of the storerooms next to the library,' Mother Dorothy said. 'We could clear one and adapt it as two cells and a lecture room. There is already a toilet up there and meditations could be done down here in the chapel. Of course the rule must be kept but I see no reason why the new arrangements wouldn't work. However this is such a novel idea that I require your opinions. Sister Hilaria?'

The novice mistress blinked her slightly protruding eyes and said, 'Yes, I approve. Bernadette and I will manage very well up there. It is quite separate from the library and far enough away from the noise of the main house not to be a distraction.'

'We're not exactly noisy over here,' Sister Perpetua objected. 'You make it sound as if we played pop music all day.'

'I meant thoughts,' Sister Hilaria said. 'Thoughts can be very loud.'

'Bernadette?' Mother Dorothy looked at her.

'I think the community needs to make money and this is a good way,' Sister Bernadette said in her decided Yorkshire accent.

'As you two are the ones most seriously affected by any change, your approval does encourage me to go ahead with a lighter heart,' Mother Dorothy said, her brow clearing. 'Has anyone any rooted objection on principle?'

'It does seem rather a pity,' Sister David hesitated, 'to lose the postulancy.'

'We won't be losing anything,' Sister Perpetua said. 'At the moment we have two people rattling about in a building designed for seven. That's waste which is against the rule anyway. We could try the lay retreat scheme for a year and then if it turns out to be a failure there's nothing lost because the postulancy is still there.'

'And by next year we may have more postulants,' Sister Hilaria said hopefully.

'Girls don't want to be nuns these days,' Sister Gabrielle said. 'If we put in a television set and let them smoke and entertain their boyfriends we'd find more of them wanting to take the veil!'

'Vocations are scarce everywhere,' Mother Dorothy said. 'At least we can comfort ourselves with the thought that quality is better than quantity.' She nodded, smiling, towards Sister Bernadette.

'Won't the alterations take some money?' Sister Katherine enquired.

'I've taken that into consideration,' Mother Dorothy informed them. 'The storerooms can be cleared and temporarily partitioned.'

'Those storerooms are crammed with stuff,' Sister Joan said. 'Some of it might be valuable.'

'I doubt that very much,' Mother Dorothy objected. 'From what I've seen of it most of the boxes are filled with junk. No, I don't propose getting rid of it. I suggest we merely move it all into the smallest of the storerooms and adapt the rest into two cells and a lecture room for Sister Hilaria and Sister Bernadette. Of course if nobody books for a retreat then they will move back into the postulancy proper and we shall have to think of some other money-making scheme.'

'What kind of retreat were you proposing to offer?' Sister Perpetua asked.

'A few quiet days in beautiful rural surroundings with good plain vegetarian food, the opportunity to relax and attend services and unwind. I was also thinking that we might give a few talks on various aspects of the cloistered life.'

'It sounds an excellent idea,' Sister Mary Concepta approved. 'I'm sure many people will be happy to come here, Reverend Mother.'

'Not without advertising they won't,' Sister Joan said.

'Isn't advertising a little vulgar?' Sister David pushed her spectacles higher on her upturned nose.

'If nobody hears about us then nobody will come,' Sister Perpetua said, allying herself with Sister Joan. 'Advertisements in the Catholic papers? In the secular Press?'

'Brochures sent out to as many parishes as we can cover,' Sister Katherine said.

'That's an excellent notion, Sisters. I have discussed this with Father Malone and he has undertaken to give it all as much publicity as possible. Am I to take it there is a general agreement then?'

'With reservations.' Sister David, who could be obstinate despite her tiny frame and rabbit features, had flushed.

'Good, then we'll set things in motion as fast as possible.' Mother Dorothy lifted a restraining hand as the sisters rose. 'Sister Joan, will you remain behind?'

'Yes, of course, Reverend Mother.' Sister Joan seated herself again. The door closed behind Sister Perpetua, the last of the line.

'Sister Joan, since you gave up duties as temporary lay sister, you must find time hangs heavily upon your hands,' the Prioress said.

'At least the cooking is better,' Sister Joan said.

'That's true,' Mother Dorothy said, looking amused. 'Your talents don't lie in the culinary field, I'm afraid. Sister Marie, on the other hand, does very well as does Sister Teresa. I did tell you some time ago that I hoped to make you assistant novice mistress. Unfortunately one postulant doesn't justify my raising you to that position. Someone, however, is required to conduct the retreats we plan. I have considered the choice very carefully and have reached the conclusion that you are the person best fitted to do so.'

'I've never run anything in my life!' Sister Joan said in alarm.

'Yours was a mature vocation,' Mother Dorothy pointed out. 'You are well acquainted with the world, Sister. You have self-confidence and plenty of good sense and you're not so spiritual as to frighten away perfectly ordinary people who come merely for a rest and don't wish to be drawn into the mystical.'

'There isn't a bit of mysticism about me,' Sister Joan agreed.

'Then you must take a look over the postulancy and see what extra furnishings will be required to make the accommodation a little more comfortable, and draw up a programme of activities and talks designed to appeal to the thoughtful lay visitor. You are, of course, at liberty to refuse the task.'

'No, of course not, Mother,' Sister Joan said, wondering what would happen if anyone ever actually refused point blank to do something the prioress wanted. 'I will certainly do my best.'

'Good.' Mother Dorothy didn't give the usual signal for departure but rested her chin on her cupped hands and gazed steadily at her junior.

'Was there something else, Reverend Mother?'

'Some post came for you yesterday,' Mother Dorothy said.

Sister Joan kept careful custody of her eyes. Even after eight years in the religious life she still felt a tremor of indignation at the thought that all correspondence in and out of the convent must be scrutinized by the prioress. Anything considered unsuitable was either withheld or censored by having the words 'apple pie' written in thick black ink over the offending portion.

'A photograph,' Mother Dorothy said. 'No accompanying letter at all. Can you think of anybody who would send you a photograph?'

'Not without a letter,' Sister Joan said.

'Well, after some consideration I have decided to give it to you, Sister.' Mother Dorothy drew a square envelope from beneath her blotter and handed it over the desk. 'I must admit I am curious.'

'Thank you, Mother.' Sister Joan sat down again, wishing that she could open the envelope when she was alone and not have to school her reaction under Mother Dorothy's sharp eyes, and drew out the glossy photograph.

There were ten of them there, frozen in an instant of time, the girls muffled in long scarves and thick jackets, the young men behind them and the wall of the art college quadrangle behind. Six girls and four young men, snapped twenty years before when the future hadn't been revealed and anything was possible.

'Sister?' Mother Dorothy's voice had an enquiring note.

'It's my class at art college,' Sister Joan said. 'There were ten of us entered as first-year students that year and we had this photograph taken sometime during the first few weeks. I haven't seen this for – I don't know how long!'

'Friends of yours. I see.'

'Classmates,' Sister Joan said. 'Oh, a few became friends but after we left college we didn't really keep up with one another. At least I didn't. We ran into one another from time to time but that's all.'

Those had been the years with Jacob who had graduated and begun earning his living while she was still struggling with life classes. Those had been the years when she had taken a variety of jobs so that she could go on sketching, learning, travelling with Jacob to the endless vistas of the Dutch horizon, to the Midi where the sky was ink-blue, to the burnt siennas of Rome.

'One day we'll go to Israel and you will see the colours there,' Jacob had said. They had never gone. By the time the idea had become feasible they knew they were unable to compromise on a mixed marriage and that parting was inevitable.

'Sister Joan?'

'I beg your pardon, Mother.' She wrenched her attention back to her superior. 'I was thinking about the past, that's all. Photographs can be powerful reminders. I'd forgotten I was ever so young!'

'At thirty-eight you're hardly in the sere and yellow,' Mother Dorothy said dryly.

'And at eighteen I was greener than anybody you ever knew!' Sister Joan said, laughing. 'We all were, I suppose. Out to conquer the world with a paintbrush and canvas. Oh!'

'Sister?' Mother Dorothy raised her eyebrows slightly.

'I beg your pardon, Mother,' Sister Joan said hastily. 'It's only that I dreamed last night that I was in a studio. Music was playing and someone was throwing paint at the walls. Perhaps I'm developing psychic abilities?'

'Do you really think so?' Mother Dorothy asked.

'No.' Sister Joan laughed again. 'This photograph was taken twenty years ago. I thought I'd forgotten all about it, but I do recall that we all agreed to meet twenty years later when we'd all be famous and terribly rich. That stayed in my subconscious, that's all.'

'Twenty years isn't such a long time. So you all planned to meet?'

'In Westminster Abbey by the tomb of Elizabeth the First.'

'I would have thought the National Gallery would have been a more appropriate venue.'

'We chose the abbey because we were all dragged there to measure the tombs and give our opinions on the styles of sculpture. Twenty years. Well, it's nice to have it. May I keep it, Mother?'

'Why was it sent to you, do you imagine?' the prioress asked.

'To remind me that we'd all agreed to meet, I suppose. Not that anyone will bother to turn up! People never do.'

'Did you keep in touch with any of them?'

'Not really,' Sister Joan admitted. 'Dodie Jones – that's the little one at the end of the front row – she sent Christmas cards for a few years and I ran into Serge Roskoff a couple of years before I entered the religious life. He was doing quite well at the time and we had a drink together. Oh, and Paul Vance does commercial work, posters, magazine covers and so on. I've seen his name occasionally. But it was all such a long time ago. I feel as if I'm talking about a different person when I look back on myself in those days.'

'Did you inform your old friends when you entered the religious life?' Mother Dorothy enquired.

'I don't think – yes, I met Fiona – she's the pretty one in the photograph – in town somewhere. We chatted for a few minutes and I told her. She was rather shocked,' Sister Joan said, her lips twitching. 'Going into a convent was equivalent in Fiona's mind to throwing oneself on to a bonfire like a Hindu widow.'

'It strikes many otherwise sensible people like that,' Mother Dorothy agreed.

'I suppose Fiona might have told some of the others,' Sister Joan volunteered. 'She was always a great chatterbox. Nobody took her very seriously as an artist I'm afraid. She was so lovely that people wanted to paint her all the time. Actually she was quite talented but her looks got in the way.'

'So someone took the trouble to find out where you are and remind you of the reunion.'

'It looks like it,' Sister Joan agreed. 'I wish they'd enclosed a note then I could have written back and made my excuses.'

'You've decided not to attend?' Mother Dorothy gave her a quizzical look.

'Mother, I'm a professed nun!' Sister Joan exclaimed. 'I can't go gadding off to college reunions.'

'Not without permission,' Mother Dorothy said.

'You'd give permission?' Sister Joan's blue eyes were incredulous.

'In normal circumstances, no,' Mother Dorothy said frankly. 'However in view of the present situation in which we are placed it might be very useful for you to meet your old friends and tell them that if they require a quiet period of rest, a recharging of their artistic batteries so to speak, then we can provide it at very moderate cost.'

'I see.' Sister Joan longed to ask if her superior had studied under Machiavelli, but contented herself with repeating, 'I see.'

'You said in Westminster Abbey. Did you decide the date and time?'

'I'm trying to remember. The photograph was taken on the fifteenth of September in the afternoon sometime – I remember it was a dull day and we weren't sure if the light was good enough and then the sun suddenly came from behind a cloud – about two on the afternoon of the fifteenth September – I think that we did joke about meeting on the same day twenty years ahead. Nobody took it too seriously.'

'Somebody did.' Mother Dorothy nodded towards the photograph.

'Evidently.' Sister Joan frowned at the young bright faces.

'So do I take it that you've requested permission to go?' Mother Dorothy asked.

'Yes, of course, Mother. I've an awful feeling that I'll probably be the only one there. And I'll certainly tell them about the retreat opportunities if anyone does turn up.'

'Good.' Mother Dorothy smiled. 'I shall see that you are provided with sufficient funds to pay for your train journey and your share of any meal. You will be returning by the late train.'

Leaving everybody else to get on with the orgy, Sister Joan thought with an inward grin as she knelt and received the blessing. Nevertheless the prospect of a day in London was an attractive one, and if she could interest a few people in the retreat scheme then that would benefit the community. Sister Joan, who frequently feared that she didn't benefit the community very much at all, went through to the kitchen with a light step to collect Alice, the Alsatian puppy acquired as a potential guard dog some time before.

Sister Teresa was scalding the dishcloths and turned a rosy, smiling face towards her. She and Sister Marie looked almost like blood sisters, each one dark-haired and pleasant-faced, already looking as if they had been brought up in convents though Sister Teresa had only just been professed and Sister Marie was in the first year of her novitiate. The latter was in the yard, mucking out Lilith's stable, and humming a hymn with as much relish as if it were a pop song.

'Alice set off without you, Sister,' Sister Teresa said. 'I put her lead on and she gave one enormous tug and was off.'

'Was she indeed?' Sister Joan tried to look stern and, failing, grinned. 'She's going to have to learn discipline or Mother Dorothy'll say she doesn't justify her keep and will have to go.'

'Over my dead body!' Sister Teresa said disrespectfully. 'Honestly, she's going to be a super dog with a bit of patience.'

'A lot,' Sister Joan corrected. 'I'd better go and find her. Thank you, Sister.'

She went out into the yard, waved to Sister Marie and turned beneath the archway towards the enclosure garden where Sister Martha was picking apples, using a long pole with a bag on the top that was about twice her own size.

It was a good harvest this year, Sister Joan mused, skirting the low wall, and reminding herself to help Sister Martha as soon as she'd found Alice. The fruit was ripe and unblighted, the currant and gooseberry bushes groaning, the vegetables bigger and crisper than ever, and the patch of corn waved golden tips in the breeze, waiting to be scythed.

She passed the cemetery where previous members of the community lay – peacefully, she hoped, though not all of them had left the world that way. At least they had had a quiet summer at the convent with nothing to disturb the tranquillity except the ever gnawing worry about money. The retreat might well bring some profit. People these days liked the idea of leaving the bustle of the world behind for a few days and finding again that central core of themselves which was so often pressed out of existence by the demands and stresses of everyday living.

It will do me good too, Sister Joan reflected as she walked across the patch of wasteland towards the steps that led down into the old tennis court. I've been like a spare part round here recently.

The trouble was that she had no specific task to occupy her. Mother Dorothy had told her to make herself useful everywhere she could but apart from driving into town to do any necessary shopping she really didn't feel she was making life easier for anyone.

The photograph was still in her pocket. Ignoring the chill wind that lifted the ends of her veil she sat down on the top step and took it out again, looking now with an unguarded face at the six girls and four youths who crouched and stood in a double line, smiling into the camera.

There was Dodie Jones, so small and prim that you knew instinctively her paintings would be as delicate and gently coloured as herself. A very private person Dodie had been, going off at the end of each term with a neat filing case full of sketches she intended to work on in the vacations. Behind her in the photograph a dark young man loomed menacingly. Derek Smith! Sister Joan bit back a smile, as she recalled the name. Derek had had the looks of an eighteenth-century pirate and the self-confidence not to change his name to anything more exotic. Paul Vance was next to him, grinning broadly as if he already knew he'd make a comfortable living in the commercial field. Paul, she remembered, had always been cheerful, a quality not always welcome on a cold morning when breakfast had been rushed and the model on the dais didn't look a bit like the figure emerging on your canvas.

Fiona crouched next to Dodie, long fair hair spilling over her shoulders, smile joyous. She'd been greatly in demand as a model when there wasn't a professional one available. Next to her was – Susan? no, Serena. Serena Clark. Plump Serena with her untidy, eye-straining fringe and a complete inability to understand the principles of perspective. Privately the others had wondered how she'd managed to get into art college until someone mentioned her father was the Samuel Clark of the wafer biscuit business and had given a large donation to the college just prior to his daughter being accepted there.

Behind Serena Serge Roskoff stood, one hand on her shoulder, his spiky fair hair looking like a wig. Serge was Russian – no, Polish or Bulgarian or something. He had been fair and quiet with nervous hands and his drawings had possessed a subtle enchantment as if Hans Christian Andersen had taken up painting instead of writing.

Bryan Grimes stood next to Serge, head thrust forward like a boxer, hands at his side. Bryan had spoken in a flat Lincolnshire accent, the expression on his stolid face never changing, and then in class at his easel had seized his brushes and made magic on a blank canvas. She'd often wondered why he hadn't made an international name for himself but perhaps he'd given up art or the muse of art had abandoned him.

Just in front of him was her own younger image, dark curly head and blue eyes that looked black in the snapshot. She had been very conscious of her slight northern accent, she remembered, and started that first day to lengthen her vowels with all the pathetic snobbishness of the young and uncertain. Next to her, almost out of the frame, was Sally Mount. She had wanted to be called Sara without the 'h', but she couldn't ever have been anyone but Sally, good-humoured even when she was being teased and probably the hardest working of them all though the results seldom justified her efforts.

Sister Joan frowned down at the picture, suddenly knowing that she didn't want to go to the stupid reunion. They had worked together in class, shared out of class coffees and wine and flirtations, that was all. They'd made no lasting friendships. No, *she* had made no lasting friendships. For all she knew there might have been closer unions formed without her being aware of them. In those days she had been eaten up with the desire to draw and paint, seeing the world and everybody in it as subjects to be captured on a rectangle of canvas or in the pages of a notebook.

And then had come Jacob, older than the others, dark and Semitic and impatient with her suburban skills.

'Don't draw the flower. Draw the essence of the flower!'

'How?' she had asked.

'By feeling it, letting it overwhelm you! Good Lord, girl, Van

Gogh didn't just paint a chair. He painted the chairness of all chairs.'

She hadn't really understood what he was telling her but she knew it was true, and she hadn't really allowed herself to sum him up, point by point, feature by feature, because it was enough to know that she loved him, would love him to the end of their lives – or at least until she had heard the sweet toned bell of the cloister and known that his faith, much as she respected it, could never be hers, and his children would have to find a different mother.

From the other side of the tennis court a rapturous Alice barked joyfully and bounded towards her. Sister Joan thrust the photograph deep in her pocket and stood up, banishing the past.

'Alice! Come on, girl! Here, girl!' Alice came, trailing her lead with a shameless air. 'You are a wretch,' Sister Joan said, slipping her hand through the loop. 'Come on! Let's go and check out the postulancy. You don't know it yet but we may be greeting visitors quite soon.'

Two

On the rare occasions Sister Joan was obliged to visit London she was always torn between excitement at the bustle all round her and nervousness as the crowds swirled past, each person seeming to know exactly where he or she was going and how to get there. Living in a convent, even one that was not entirely enclosed, was rather like living in some long-term institution, she thought wryly, keeping a close eye on the names of the stations as the Tube train screamed through tunnels and doors opened and closed, engorging and disgorging passengers. The train itself was fairly full but not uncomfortably so. She had noticed with a feeling of mingled amusement and hurt that the space next to her had remained unoccupied. People still hesitated before sitting next to a nun.

'I don't believe it!' A slim, dark woman, her hair drawn back into a French pleat, her beautifully cut suit of dark-green velvet complementing her colouring had stopped and was staring down at Sister Joan, a smile curving her lightly painted mouth.

Sister Joan stared back blankly, the beginnings of embarrassment tinting her throat as she racked her memory for a name to put to the face. It was always dreadful to run into someone you couldn't recall, insulting to them somehow.

'Barbara,' the woman said, lowering herself into the empty space next to Sister Joan. 'Barbara Ford.'

'Good heavens!' Sister Joan said, forgetting tact in the force of her surprise. 'I'd never have recognized you!'

Barbara had been at college too, but had left after the second term, called home to nurse a dying father. During her time there she had made so little impression that it wasn't until several days after she'd gone, moving out silently and with no fuss, that anyone had noticed. And then it had been one of the tutors who had told them the reason. Barbara herself had confided in nobody. She had come and gone like a pale grey shadow, seldom initiating a conversation, always crouching over an easel in the corner where she worked with irritating slowness and produced work as forgettable as herself.

'You haven't changed at all,' Barbara said, apparently not taking offence at the remark. 'I'd have known you anywhere. But then nuns never look old, do they?'

Barbara had been prone to make vague generalizations on the rare occasions she'd ventured an opinion, Sister Joan remembered. She had worn a shabby smock and jeans and tied back her hair in a tight ponytail. Brown hair surely, not this gleaming black.

'I dyed my hair,' Barbara said as if she'd just intercepted the other's glance. 'To tell you the truth I always wanted hair your colour – that lovely blue-black!'

'It suits you,' Sister Joan said truthfully. 'You look lovely.'

'Thank you.' Barbara inclined her head slightly.

'But what are you doing in—? Oh, this is my stop! Can you—?'

'It's my stop too,' Barbara said, rising and making for the door in one swift fluid movement.

On the platform Sister Joan said, 'You're going to the Abbey too?'

'Someone sent me a copy of the photograph,' Barbara said.

Sister Joan opened her mouth to say, 'But you weren't on it!' and had the sense to close it again as they made for the stairs, Barbara bringing out the shiny snapshot and holding it under her nose, one well-manicured figure pointing at the vague figure next to Dodie Jones.

'I must have moved slightly,' Barbara said. 'It's a bit of a blur.'

'Yes.'

She hadn't even noticed the figure at the end, never allowed the thin outline, the faint impression on features to register on her consciousness. It had been the same in class or in the lecture hall. Barbara had simply disappeared into the general background. Even at the pub when they were all relaxed and laughing almost inevitably someone had had to go to the bar and get Barbara's forgotten drink.

'Did you send the photo?' Barbara asked, putting it away as they emerged into the daylight.

'You didn't?'

'No. I'd forgotten all about it. In fact I don't think I ever had a copy of it. I remembered what we'd arranged, of course, when it came.'

'One of the others must've sent it,' Sister Joan said. 'Have you met any of them since you left?'

'I saw Derek Smith on a late-night television chat show a couple of years ago,' Barbara said. 'Of course I didn't finish the course – my father—'

'Yes, we were very sorry to hear,' Sister Joan began.

'Father didn't die.' Was there a hint of amusement in the clear grey eyes? 'He was very ill, of course, for a long time, but he eventually recovered. It would have been possible for me to take up my studies again but I felt the right time had gone past.'

'And he's still well?'

'He remarried and went to New Zealand,' Barbara said.

If she resented being discarded the moment her filial devotion was no longer necessary she gave no sign of it.

'And yourself?' Sister Joan hoped that Barbara hadn't made a name for herself in art circles or something equally embarrassing not to know.

'I went out to New Zealand with them – with father and Claire. That's the woman he married. She's very nice. About five years ago I came back to England. I've got a good job in public relations now.'

'It sounds important.'

'Not really but it's interesting and well paid. Do you still paint? I mean are you allowed—?'

'Now and then I'm given permission,' Sister Joan said, sounding more resigned than she often felt.

'I suppose the praying doesn't leave much time for anything else,' Barbara said, sending her a sympathetic look.

'Oh, we manage to fit everything in,' Sister Joan said cheerfully. 'Even nuns have to earn some kind of living for the sake of the community. In fact we're branching out a bit; we're going to run a series of weekend and week-long retreats – you know, holidays for people who want a peaceful few days without any stress or strain.'

Listening to herself she thought uneasily that she sounded like a walking advertisement for convents, but Barbara looked interested.

'It sounds like an awfully good idea,' she said warmly. 'You must tell the others about it. I mean, if any of us have a few free days we could all book in together and carry on the reunion!'

'If there are any others here,' Sister Joan said, pausing briefly as they entered the Abbey so the security guard could conduct a cursory inspection.

'We'll have to wait and see,' Barbara said, lowering her voice in deference to the sacredness of the place. 'Do you remember exactly where in the Abbey we were supposed to meet up?'

'By the tomb of Elizabeth the First.'

'Yes, of course! Did you see the Glenda Jackson series? Wasn't it splendid? Of course, I suppose you prefer Queen Mary, being a Catholic and all.'

'Not really.' Sister Joan felt a tiny spasm of irritation. 'I never had much time for religious fanatics. Burning my fellow men and women at the stake never struck me as the best way of getting converts.'

'I suppose not. We live in more tolerant times,' Barbara said.

Sister Joan bit her lip, repressing the impulse to retort that toleration of some things like cruelty and prejudice was just as undesirable. She was remembering more and more how Barbara Ford had been like a pale, insignificant insect that could hover and swoop in a maddening fashion.

A tall, dark man was striding towards them, hands outstretched, white teeth gleaming under a close-clipped moustache.

'Joan and – Barbara!' There was the merest flicker of hesitation before he spoke the second name. 'I was starting to imagine this was some damned practical joke! How are you both? You look absolutely marvellous! You've forgotten me?'

'Nobody could ever forget you, Derek,' Sister Joan said, amused, shaking hands.

'Once seen never forgotten, eh?' He flung an arm about each of them as they walked on beneath the echoing stone. 'Which one of you sent the photo?'

'Neither of us,' Barbara said. 'You didn't?'

Derek shook his head. 'I'd shoved all the old college stuff in a suitcase and forgotten about it,' he said. '*Tempus fugit* and all that. You'll know the Latin better than I do, Joan – or is it Sister Someone or Other now?'

'Sister Joan. Whenever possible we keep our own Christian names in the order.'

'In the order!' His eyes glinted as he repeated the phrase. 'Of all the girls at college you're the very last one I'd imagine would run into a convent. Which order are you in anyway? Not Carmelite or Poor Clare! Not in a grey habit.'

'Daughters of Compassion,' she told him. 'It was founded during the war by a Dutch girl who died in a concentration camp. After her death it was given the official seal of approval from the Vatican.'

'And they let you out?'

'Now and then,' she said demurely. 'Of course we're all electronically tagged in case we leave the country.'

'You're joking, aren't you?' Barbara's perfectly made-up face betrayed a shadow of anxiety.

'I'm joking,' Sister Joan said.

'And what about you, Barbara? Married? Divorced?'

'Single,' Barbara said.

'Wish I'd known,' Derek said, heaving a sigh as he dropped his arms from their shoulders. 'If I'd realized you were going to blossom into a beauty I'd have kept tags on you, believe you me!'

'What about yourself? Are you married?' Sister Joan asked.

'You didn't hear?' For an instant the laughter shrivelled at the back of his eyes. 'I married Sally – you remember Sally Mount?'

Pleasant, plump, good-natured Sally with her attempts to draw something that would earn one word of praise from her tutor. Sister Joan thought fleetingly that of all of them she'd have chosen nice, ordinary Sally Mount as the one least likely to be chosen by Derek Smith.

'Sally was always very nice to me,' Barbara said.

'She's not with you?' Sister Joan stopped abruptly, deciding that if he had married Sally it was unlikely the marriage had lasted. Derek had always been the one eager for new experiences, eager to move on, deciding one term that Dali was the only artist worth studying, the next term arriving with a boisterous enthusiasm for Renoir.

'She died,' Derek said.

'Died!' Sister Joan automatically blessed herself. 'Derek, I'm so sorry! She was always so – full of energy, so healthy. I'm really very sorry.'

'She wasn't sick.' He had paused, reaching out to caress the outlines of a tiny gargoyle carved on a pillar. 'She fell.'

'Fell?' Barbara echoed the word.

'A couple of years ago. She was in a multistorey car-park,' he said. 'One of those towering blocks of steel and stone with openings all round. She had parked the car there and she must have gone over to look out – she was always keen on views – and fallen out.'

'Surely there was a guard rail or something!' Sister Joan exclaimed.

'There was, but it was low. There had been a couple of complaints and the council had promised to do something about it. There were temporary wooden barriers up, but Sally must have stepped round one and leaned out to get a better view. It was an accident.'

He sounded as if he were forbidding speculation.

'Someone saw it?' Barbara asked the question that Sister Joan wanted to ask.

Derek ran his hand down the pillar with a small scraping sound.

'It was late afternoon,' he said. 'Just after the rush hour. The lights in the streets were just being switched on. Sally loved the lights, the patterns they made – she must've gone over to look down at them. The irony of it is that I'd offered to go shopping with her but she wanted to buy me a birthday present and insisted on going alone. Death through misadventure. I went abroad for a bit to wander about, get over it. Which I did, of course.'

'That's terribly sad,' Barbara said. 'We're both so sorry. Aren't we, Joan?'

'It's over. These things sometimes happen. No need to make a federal case out of it,' Derek said gruffly.

'Well, we're very sorry anyway,' Barbara said, touching his

arm lightly. 'Had you any family?'

'We decided not,' Derek said, beginning to walk on again. 'My career was taking off in a fairly big way and Sally was terribly good at all the business side of it. Arranging the exhibitions, checking contracts, you know.'

And that was why he had probably married her in the beginning, Sister Joan mused, as they walked slowly on. Sally hadn't had an ounce of talent worth cultivating but that meant she wouldn't have provided any competition. She'd have worshipped at the shrine of her brilliant husband and counted herself lucky to be his wife. Yet had she been truly content? Leaning out of a multistorey car-park in order to get a better view of the lighted panorama of streets beneath struck her as an odd thing to do.

'Well, here's the tomb,' Barbara said, breaking the silence that had fallen. The elaborate tomb of Elizabeth of England was separated only by the nave from that of the Queen of Scots, buried almost within spitting distance of each other, Sister Joan thought with a twinge of amusement, and jumped slightly as a figure emerged from the side of the stone catafalque and stood, regarding them with head tipped slightly to one side.

'You won't remember me,' Dodie Jones said in her breathless little voice.

'Who could forget our Dodie?' Derek stepped forward and enveloped her in a bear hug from which she emerged, slightly flushed, straightening the unfashionable beanie hat stuck at the back of her greying head.

Dodie hadn't changed, Sister Joan thought, joining in the greetings. She had always been slim, small and neat, much given to Peter Pan collars and oak-leaf brooches and barely-there lipstick. Now her face was slightly lined, her indeterminate hair colour faded to grey, but the essence of Dodie was all there.

'I wondered who had sent me the photograph,' she was saying. 'I'd remembered about it, of course, and I'd warned Colin that I might be deserting the nest for a day – Colin's my husband.'

'You married?' Sister Joan couldn't keep the surprise out of her voice.

'We had our fifteenth anniversary in June,' Dodie said. 'He's an engineer. We live in Maidstone. Two children. Simon is twelve and Cecily ten, both at boarding-school, so Colin and I are a twosome again.'

She smiled at them, each tooth small, white, perfectly even. There was something smug about Dodie. There always had been, Sister Joan thought. Dodie had never been late for class, never stayed up late drinking and setting the world to rights with her tongue. Dodie had been elderly in her teens.

'Of course I'm Dodie Mason now,' she was saying. 'Tell me about the rest of you. Derek, I heard about Sally, of course, and sent a card. It was very sad. Barbara, I heard a rumour you'd emigrated to New Zealand. Are you back for good now?'

'Probably. I'm really not sure,' Barbara said.

'And you became a nun.' Dodie had turned to Sister Joan. 'You look about twenty-five, honestly! Doesn't she look about twenty-five, Barbara?'

'It's leading a pure life,' Sister Joan said ironically.

'And you don't get cancer either, do you? I read about it,' Dodie said, missing the irony completely.

'Oh, you mustn't believe everything you read,' Sister Joan said lightly.

'It looks as if we're the only ones who are going to turn up.' Derek consulted a handsome watch on his tanned wrist.

'Surely someone else will,' Sister Joan objected. 'The one who sent out the photos isn't likely to miss the reunion.'

'Well, it doesn't seem to have been one of us,' Dodie said, looking at them. 'Did any of you get a letter? There was no letter with mine.'

'Just the photograph,' Barbara said, glancing at the other two who nodded.

'Here comes the possible culprit!' Derek said, half turning to watch a plump woman wend her way towards them.

'It's Serena,' Dodie said.

It couldn't have been anyone but Serena, with her fringe still untidy and streaked with grey, her overflowing flesh inadequately corseted, her fringed scarf trailing over her shoulder and catching in the strap of her outsize shoulder bag. Serena was Serena yet after twenty years. She was shaking hands now, rings flashing fire against the dark surrounding stone.

'Well, but this is marvellous! You all look wonderful! I've been so excited ever since I received the photograph, trying to picture if you'd all have changed.'

'You didn't send the photograph?' Barbara queried.

'No.' Serena shook her head, pushing back her fringe in an old familiar gesture.

'None of us did,' Dodie said. 'Well, we're all here nearly, aren't we? You, Barbara, Sister Joan, myself, Derek.'

'That's only five people,' Serena said.

'Yes, but Sally won't be here,' Barbara said tactlessly.

'You and Sally got divorced? I'm on my second divorce at the moment. Hellish, aren't they?' Serena said.

'Sally died a couple of years ago,' Derek told her. 'You hadn't heard?'

'Not a word. Seth – that's my soon-to-be ex-husband – and I went off on a world cruise year before last. An ill-fated attempt to patch up our differences, which didn't work though the holiday was brilliant,' Serena said. 'I'm awfully sorry. I liked Sally. Wasn't she terribly young to die?'

'It was an accident,' Derek said.

'Oh, that is sad!' Serena looked moistly concerned. 'I mean it's always sad when anyone dies, but you can't help getting ill, whereas when it's an accident there's always an if only – you know!'

'You mean if only Sally hadn't leaned out from the top of a multistorey car-park she might not have lost her balance and tumbled out?' Derek said with sudden flat brutality.

'Is that what happened? Oh, I do think some of those places are dreadfully dangerous!' Serena exclaimed. 'I thought you were going to say it was a crash – like Bryan Grimes.'

'Bryan Grimes has been in a car crash?' Sister Joan said. 'What happened? Is he all right?'

'Well, he's dead,' Serena said calmly. 'I don't know if that means he's all right now or not. I mean it depends on your views about the afterlife.'

'Never mind about the afterlife!' Barbara said impatiently. 'What happened?'

'There was a hit-and-run-accident,' Serena said. 'A drunk driver probably or a joyrider, though I do think that's a silly name to call them. I mean they don't provide much joy, do they? Anyway I happened to read a bit about it in the newspaper. Only a column which seems rather a pity when one remembers how clever Bryan was! He was living back in Lincolnshire, near Boston, I believe, and he must've been taking a walk or something because someone ran over him and didn't stop. I knew it was the Bryan we knew because it mentioned that he illustrated children's books.'

'When did this happen?' Derek asked sharply.

'Last year sometime. Let me see – Seth and I decided to call it a day in March, so it must have been just after that – April? Yes, April, when I read about it. I did wonder if I ought to go to the funeral or write to somebody but we hadn't kept in touch since college or anything – did anyone else keep in touch?'

'If we had then we'd have known he was dead,' Dodie pointed out.

'Was he married?' Barbara asked.

'It didn't mention any widow,' Serena said. 'Perhaps he was gay.'

'Of course Bryan wasn't gay,' Barbara said crossly. 'Just because a man isn't married at thirty-seven doesn't mean he's gay.'

'Whatever he was he was a nice person,' Sister Joan said. 'I'm sorry to hear the news.'

'So Bryan couldn't have sent the photograph,' Dodie said. 'That leaves Paul, Fiona and Serge. Paul might have sent it.'

'You can ask him yourself,' Derek said, nodding towards an approaching figure in cotton sweater and jeans as if it were still high summer.

'I'm late but I had some work to catch up on!' Paul shook hands, perspiration on his receding hairline. 'Hey! I'd have known you anywhere, Dodie, Joan. Barbara, you've gone glamorous on us! Serena, nice to see you! Really nice to see you all! Why the grim faces? I wasn't that late was I?'

'We just heard about Sally and Bryan,' Sister Joan said.

'I knew about Sally. Hard luck that, old man!' Paul clapped Derek on the shoulder. 'I meant to write but you know how it is – time goes on! Anyway, somewhat belated condolences! Sally was a nice girl. What did you want to ask me?'

'Ask—? Oh, did you send round copies of the photograph to remind us of the reunion?' Barbara asked.

'No. Mine arrived about a week ago. Posted in London.'

'I never thought to look where mine was posted from.' Sister Joan took out the square envelope and looked at the postmark. 'London too.'

'And mine,' said Dodie. 'I said to Colin when it came, "Now who on earth is writing to me from London? It's years since I was there".'

'Mine was posted in London too,' Barbara said. 'W.1.'

'Mine too,' Derek said. 'Not that it means much. Well, that leaves Fiona or Serge, neither of whom has turned up yet.'

'You can bet it wasn't Fiona,' Paul said. 'That girl never knew the time of the next lecture. She certainly wouldn't remember a reunion planned twenty years ago!'

'There's no sign of anyone else coming,' Dodie said.

'And you must all be getting hungry!' Serena exclaimed, adding, 'I'm actually slimming at the moment so I won't need more than a snack, but the rest of you must feel quite peckish!'

'Still slimming?' Dodie said, a little smile lifting her mouth. 'Honestly, Serena, I'd have thought that after twenty years you'd have given it up as a bad job by now!'

'We'll all eat,' Barbara said, 'except for Dodie who'll enjoy a nice saucer of milk. It's way past two so I vote we repair to the nearest café and catch up on the past few years.'

'And not wait for Serge and Fiona?' Paul nodded. 'Good idea. No guarantee that either of them'll turn up.'

'But one of them must have sent the photo,' Dodie protested.

'Then they should've been on time. Come on, Joan – or is it Sister now?'

'Joan sounds fine.'

'Sister Joan,' Barbara said, shaking her head as they drifted back to the door. 'I never knew you'd become a nun, Joan. I thought you went off and married that Jewish fellow – Jacob or something.'

She had known, of course, that sooner or later the name would be spoken in just such a casual way, and had expected to feel pain, but the pain was muted now as if it had all happened before to a different person.

'Oh, we did talk about it,' she said equably, 'but neither of us could make the final commitment and then, for me, at least, something better came along.'

'Better than sex?' Serena looked astonished.

'Different,' Sister Joan said.

'How long have you been a nun?' Barbara enquired.

'Eight years. Mine was what they call a late vocation.'

'And they let you in even after – you know – lost your virginity?'

'Actually they never asked.' Sister Joan interrupted Dodie's prim little voice. 'They didn't ask if I'd lost it, sold it, lent it or given it away. They're not as fixated on physical details as people outside seem to think. And for me different turned out a whole lot better.'

'Do you ever hear from Jacob?' Barbara came to her side as they emerged into the bright afternoon sunshine.

'Not a word,' Sister Joan said.

'I heard he'd gone back to Israel,' Derek volunteered. 'Mind you, I think I only met him once or twice. Where shall we eat?'

'We could get the boat down to the Tower and have a lovely English tea in the restaurant there,' Serena said.

'It's a bit early for tea,' Paul said.

'Speak for yourself! I missed lunch. When does the next boat go?'

'Three o'clock, I think. Let's go and look at Westminster Hall,' Barbara suggested.

'What's to see?' Derek said.

'The architecture,' Barbara said. 'It's either that or hang round the abbey and that's a bit overwhelming as far as I'm concerned. Come on!'

She plunged across the road towards the building, leaving the others trailing in her wake.

'Our Barbara's blossomed out quite a bit, hasn't she?' Paul said, looking after her with amusement. 'She used to be one of the most colourless people I knew.'

'We all change, I suppose,' Sister Joan said.

'Not you, dear! You haven't aged at all.'

'That's because I'm a nun,' Sister Joan said with resignation.

'Cheaper than a facelift, eh? So what's this about Bryan then? Someone said he was dead. Last I heard he was illustrating children's books back in Lincolnshire.'

'Apparently there was a hit and run accident last year. I only just heard about it and about Sally's death myself. I was very sorry.'

'Ditto.' He sounded casual, uncaring. 'Mind you, I hadn't seen anyone for ages. My own work takes up a lot of time.'

'I used to see your designs on television sometimes,' she told him. 'You've done really well, haven't you?'

'Commercially.' He shrugged dismissively, his thin, sharp face betraying discontent.

They were in the soaring space of Westminster Hall. It was years since she'd stood here, looking at the steps on which men whose names were recorded in history had pleaded their cases. Here Raleigh had defended himself, calling to witness the late queen, that 'lady whom Time hath forgot'. Here St Thomas More had flung defiance at the king.

Within her short white veil her round face was thoughtful.

'There you are! All of you! I've been waiting for ages, simply ages!'

A slim blonde vision was threading her way through a little group of Japanese tourists who left off looking at the stone and gaped at her instead as she undulated towards the others, hands outstretched, short skirt revealing magnificent legs. People had always turned to look at Fiona, Sister Joan thought, jerked back into the present as the other flung her arms round her as if they had been bosom friends.

'Joan! Oh, but you're dressed up as a nun!'

'That's because I am one,' Sister Joan said, amused.

'Honestly?' Fiona opened her turquoise eyes still wider and fell back a step. 'I never knew. Nobody ever tells me anything! Were you disappointed in love or aren't you allowed to tell? Dodie, how super to see you! You look wonderful. Doesn't she look wonderful everybody? I've been here ages honestly. After I got the photograph I remembered about the reunion, of course, but maybe I got the time wrong?'

'Not the time but the place,' Barbara told her. 'We were supposed to meet in the abbey itself by the tomb of Queen Elizabeth.'

'Were we?' Fiona looked even blanker, then laughed. 'Oh, well, never mind! We're all here now! Are we going for a drink or something? Catch up on the last twenty years?'

'Serge Roskoff isn't here,' Derek said.

'And he must have been the one who sent out all the photographs.' Dodie nodded as if she'd just solved an important mystery.

'Well, he's not here,' Barbara said impatiently. 'I honestly don't see much point in waiting much longer. I vote we get the boat down to the Tower and have something to eat there.'

'The Tower? Oh, oh wonderfully spooky!' Fiona linked her arm through Paul's, glancing up at him through the naturally dark eyelashes that contrasted with the naturally fair hair brushing her shoulders.

It was a teasing, flirtatious glance which should have looked ridiculous on a woman of nearly forty, but it looked charming. Fiona had only the faintest of lines at the corners of her eyes to prove she was no longer eighteen, and she hadn't put on a pound of spare flesh since Sister Joan had seen her last. If I wasn't a religious, Sister Joan thought, with a tremor of amusement, I'd be dead jealous!

They were streaming towards the wharf to join the queue for the boat that would take them at a leisurely pace down the Thames past various landmarks pointed out by the guide over the loudspeaker. There wouldn't be time for any private conversation. Sister Joan paid for her ticket and took her seat on the wooden bench, Dodie squeezing in next to her.

'She must've had a facelift,' Dodie was whispering. 'Honestly her whole body is simply defying gravity!'

'I don't think so,' Sister Joan murmured back. 'She looks absolutely natural to me.'

There was no need to ask whom Dodie was talking about.

'We're far too late for lunch,' Serena was proclaiming, 'but since I seldom eat any it's the rest of you I'm worrying about.'

'Do you get lunch in the convent?' Barbara enquired.

'Soup and a sandwich – vegetarian,' Sister Joan told her.

'Is it a terribly strict order?'

'Middling.'

Why, she wondered, did convent life fascinate lay people so much? She'd been much the same herself once, she supposed, though she hoped she hadn't held such silly ideas about the cloistered life. Semi-cloistered in her case. The river flowing past the boat was greenish-grey. She shut out the surrounding noises and drifted with it.

'Does anyone know where Serge lives these days?' Dodie was asking. 'We could all go round and get him if he lives in London.'

'As a matter of fact I know,' Paul said unexpectedly, leaning forward as the boat scraped against the wharf. 'At least I know where he hung out six months ago. He had an exhibition in one of the smaller galleries and I saw it advertised. I did think that it might make a bit of an item on the arts programme, so I got my agent to find out his address. Flat Fifteen, Putney Walk – somewhere near the Embankment. Anyway I dropped him a line but he never bothered to answer.'

'Sounds like Serge,' Derek commented. 'He was always a moody sod.'

They disembarked, nodding thanks to the guide to whose spiel nobody had troubled to listen. On their left the high walls of the Tower loomed up.

'This is rather a grim place for a reunion,' Serena complained, dragging her scarf clear of her bag. 'First the Abbey and then the Tower! Why not the Chamber of Horrors at Madame Tussaud's?'

'We probably provide quite sufficient horror all by ourselves,' Barbara said.

'A bunch of old fogies trying to recapture their youth.' Paul was nodding.

'Who's calling whom an old fogy?' Fiona demanded.

'Nobody,' Serena said. 'Paul's being sarcastic as usual.'

'Paul's being truthful,' Paul said. 'I don't really mean we're old fogies exactly! None of us is past forty yet after all, but these reunions, years after most of us have lost touch and gone our separate ways – it's a bit pathetic.'

'I think it's lovely,' Dodie said. 'Meeting old friends and catching up on all the news. Let's go and have something to eat and then we can go round and drag Serge out for the evening! It's only fair he should join in since he obviously set the whole thing up!'

Three

'I suggest we take turns and give a brief resumé of what we've been doing since college,' Barbara said.

They were drinking coffee after smoked salmon sandwiches and white wine. Sister Joan felt a pleasant sense of dissipation as she sipped her drink. So far talk had been desultory, odd remarks tossed into the air, caught or dropped.

'We'd be here all night,' Fiona objected.

'You might be, darling,' Paul said, 'since we all know you lead a very, very busy life but Dodie won't take more than two minutes flat, will you?'

'You start, Barbara,' Sister Joan said.

'My account really will take two minutes,' Barbara said deprecatingly. 'I had to give up college in my second term because father was so gravely ill, and by the time he was well again I just didn't feel like going back. Anyway he'd met a very lovely lady. Claire's a nurse, over here then from New Zealand on an exchange scheme, so they got married and we went to New Zealand. I went to business school out there, got a good job, worked my way up. Five years ago I was offered a promotion. It entailed a transfer over here so I decided to return.'

'Looking extremely smart, if I may say so,' Derek said.

'Thank you.' For an instant, as she smiled, a trace of the shy, colourless Barbara they had scarcely noticed, appeared, and then was gone.

'No private life?' Dodie's tip-tilted nose twitched slightly.

'The occasional fling.' Barbara drank her coffee.

'If anyone were to hear my personal history,' Serena said, 'they simply wouldn't credit it! They wouldn't!'

'Just give us an outline,' Derek said, winking at the others.

'Well, let's see.' Serena pushed back her fringe and concentrated. 'Of course I never was any good at drawing or painting, but Daddy had money so I got in. I daresay that was unfair but it didn't honestly bother me. I mean I hope I didn't keep a better student out or anything but—'

'We knew you had a rich daddy,' Paul said. 'Get on with what happened after you left. You didn't get your qualifications, did you?'

'I scraped through,' Fiona said.

'I didn't even manage that,' Serena said cheerfully. 'Daddy couldn't pull any more strings. I didn't mind. It was fun being a student, that's all. And I didn't have to work anyway. So it didn't matter. I did the social bit – Claridges, Queen Charlotte's Ball, Ascot, all that. Then I got married. He was rather sweet actually but no brains and not much money. Anyway I stuck it out for ten years and then we had an amicable divorce. I went abroad for a bit – the hippie trail—'

'Weren't you a bit late for that?' Sister Joan said.

'I'm usually late for things,' Serena said, tugging at her fringe again. 'I mean as soon as I get round to buying the latest fashion it goes out of fashion. Anyway I meandered about a bit and then I met Seth. He's a professional polo player, not terribly famous but handsome and awfully good company, so we got married about four years ago. It didn't work out very well. He turned out to be rather greedy. Anyway we took a cruise a couple of years ago and tried to patch things up, but it didn't really work out so we decided to get divorced. It's been hanging on a bit because the lawyers keep trying to hold on to my money for me. I tell them it really doesn't matter because I'm quite happy for Seth to have as much as he wants but Daddy left everything tied up in trusts and things and it takes forever to disentangle. Seth and I just wait.'

'No family?' Dodie asked.

'No, nothing ever came along,' Serena said. 'Daddy would have liked a grandchild but I never was the maternal type. It just didn't happen.'

'I have two children,' Dodie said. 'Simon is twelve and Cecily is ten. They're both at boarding-school.'

'Any husband?' Paul enquired.

'Of course I have a husband!' Two circles of colour dyed her cheeks. 'Colin is an engineer and we've been married for fifteen years. After we left college I got a job designing greetings cards, and one day I saw him buying one of my designs so I couldn't resist telling him I was the artist. We got talking and that was it really.'

'And do you still design greetings cards, dear?' Paul asked.

'From time to time. It brings in a little extra – not that Colin can't support me! He's done awfully well. But it's nice to have a bit of money for myself and, of course, I can do my cards in my spare time when the children are away or at school.'

'You turned commercial,' Paul said.

'Yes, just like you,' Dodie answered. The gleam in her smile was razor sharp.

'I defy anyone to live on nothing while you're waiting for some critic to notice that what you're doing is worth writing about!' he retorted. 'Serena didn't have to bother; Barbara went into a profession that suited her better, and you – you found yourself a meal ticket so you could've held out a bit longer. You actually had some real talent.'

'So did you,' Derek said. 'You ended up designing logos for commercials.'

'Which is a highly competitive business,' Paul said. 'At least I'm communicating with the public, and earning very high fees. Once I get my name known internationally in the commercial field then I can paint something worthwhile without having to fret about the overdraft.'

'You've still got an overdraft after all this time?' Fiona looked amazed.

'I've work contracted that has to be done before I can start doing the kind of thing I want to do,' Paul said defensively.

'Did you get married?' Sister Joan asked.

Paul's sharp dark eyes moved to her face and rested there. 'Don't be naïve, Sister dear,' he said.

'Oh.' Sister Joan felt a blush rising. 'You mean you're – I didn't know.'

'I never made a song and dance about it,' Paul said. 'Twenty years ago it wasn't the done thing to come roaring out of the closet. I'd have thought you guessed though.'

'I was more interested in my own love life than anyone

else's,' she confessed.

'Well, I never had a love life as such. Nothing permanent,' he said.

'It sounds a bit like me,' Fiona said.

'You're gay?' Derek stared at her.

'No, of course not,' Fiona said, giggling. 'No, I meant that I never met the right man, that's all. Plenty of wrong ones but too many to list right now.'

'What about your painting?' Sister Joan asked.

'I never did very much,' Fiona said.

'That's because you were always being called on to model,' Serena said. 'Did you take it up professionally?'

Fiona shook her head, the wings of fair hair swinging forward to cover her perfectly moulded cheekbones.

'I went abroad,' she said. 'The States first, where I got a small part in a long running soap, and then an aunt died and left me some money – not your kind of money, Serena, but enough to live on if I'm careful. I teach art now part-time. That's all really. Not very exciting.'

'I daresay you left out the juicy bits,' Dodie said. 'Derek?'

'I'm still painting.' He sounded abrupt. 'Unlike Paul and Dodie I didn't sell my soul to commercialism, though I have opened a fine arts shop to supplement my earnings. I get some excellent reviews but these days nobody buys paintings until you're dead.'

'They never did,' Paul said. 'You got married, didn't you?'

'Sixteen years ago, just after we left college. I met up with Sally and we fell for each other. Funny really because I scarcely noticed her in college. Anyway we got married and Sally took over all the business side of things. I relied on her.'

'And then she died,' Dodie said.

'How?' Fiona looked from face to face.

'She fell out of the top storey of a multistorey car-park a couple of years ago,' he said coldly. 'Accident.'

'And Bryan Grimes was killed by a hit-and-run driver in Lincolnshire last year,' Dodie said.

'I can't even remember Bryan,' Fiona remarked.

'You ought to,' Barbara said abruptly. 'You were sleeping with him at college.'

'Was I?' Fiona opened her eyes wider, then screwed them shut.

'You can't expect her to remember names, my darlings,' Paul mocked.

'It was a long time ago,' Fiona said vaguely. 'If Barbara says I did then I'm sure she's right. He illustrated children's books, didn't he? I do remember that.'

'They all look alike in the dark,' Dodie said.

'I wouldn't have thought you'd ever have had the chance to find out,' Paul said.

'I don't mind,' Fiona said. 'It's only Dodie's teasing.'

'Has Joan told you about her weekend retreats?' Barbara interposed.

'Retreat from where?' Fiona enquired.

'From stress and strain in the workaday world,' Sister Joan said, feeling as if she had suddenly been thrust into the limelight. 'It's a new venture for us actually, to help pay our way.'

'Don't you get a grant from Rome?' Dodie asked.

'From your mouth to God's ear!' Spontaneously she used an old phrase of Jacob's she hadn't remembered for years. 'No, we don't get any grants from anywhere. We're expected to support ourselves – each house in the Order of the Daughters of Compassion is self-supporting.'

'What kind of work do you all do?' Serena asked.

'At present, various jobs. We sell garden produce in the local market and Sister Katherine makes lace and Sister David does translations into Latin and Greek and she's preparing a series of books about the saints for children.'

'What's your job?' Derek asked.

'I'm a bit of a jack of all trades,' Sister Joan said ruefully. 'I used to teach in a little local school but it had to close when the council provided transport for the local children into Bodmin. After that I was acting lay sister for a bit—'

'Why not paint?' Paul interrupted.

'Mother Dorothy, that's our prioress, hasn't given her permission yet.'

'Then Mother Dorothy wants telling!' he said brusquely.

'Where is this convent?' Fiona wanted to know.

'Obviously in Cornwall,' Dodie said snubbingly.

'On the moors,' Sister Joan said, wishing suddenly she was back there. 'The estate used to belong to an important family and the order acquired it after the last of them. It's a lovely old house set in large grounds with a dower-house in the garden. That's what we use as the postulancy but as we only have one postulant at the moment we've turned it into a guesthouse for visitors.'

'Are you sure you're not trying to get more postulants?' Fiona asked with another giggle.

'That would be nice,' Sister Joan said, 'but not very practical. No, we're hoping to provide a series of short breaks at a reasonable price with walks in the neighbourhood, access to the library – we've got a good library, a fairly free and easy time in fact.'

'We're none of us Catholics,' Dodie said.

'That's not important. You can join in the daily worship or not just as you please.'

'Can you smoke there?' Serena asked.

'In the guesthouse sitting-room,' Sister Joan assured her, bending the rules on impulse. 'The food's vegetarian but nearly all home grown. Sister Teresa is an excellent cook.'

'How many of you are there?' Dodie enquired.

'Ten fully professed, one novice and one postulant. Actually we're a pretty lively bunch.'

'And you've been sent out to do the advertising? You've turned commercial too!' Paul said.

'You know it might be rather fun!' Barbara exclaimed. 'After twenty years one day isn't enough to get everything said. Why don't we all band together and come for a few days?'

'We only have seven cells – rooms,' she protested.

'Cells! How delicious!' Fiona gave an exaggerated shiver. 'Couldn't two of us share?'

'One room is larger than the others,' Sister Joan said, measuring in her mind. 'If two people did share then they could come for half-price.'

'I take it you'll be sleeping over in the guesthouse?' Dodie looked at her.

'I'll share with you,' Fiona said brightly. 'Honestly I don't mind if you don't.'

'It'll make a lovely change for you, won't it, Fiona?' Dodie said waspishly.

Sister Joan bit her lip. Funny how in her memory they had all been so much nicer! Young and eager and ready to laugh, not malicious, sniping. If it wasn't for the fact that the convent needed the money she'd be tempted to tell them all to take a running jump at something or other!

'Fiona can share with me,' Serena said placidly. 'Do you have any details about dates and so on?'

'There's going to be a brochure but it's not ready yet,' Sister Joan said. 'I can give you the prospective dates of the first retreat though. It lasts for a week. Oh, and the phone number of the convent. Then it's up to you to book if you like.'

'We can fix it all up over dinner,' Barbara said. 'Try to find a week when we're all free.'

'Sorry but I can't.' Sister Joan squinted at the steel fob watch pinned to her habit and dug in her deep pocket for her purse. 'I have to be back in the convent before the grand silence. You sort out among yourselves what you want to do, and give the convent a ring. The first retreat runs from the second to the eighth of October, but anyone's welcome to come on the previous day since transport isn't awfully frequent on a Sunday.'

'Wouldn't it be better to start it on the Saturday anyway?' Barbara said. 'Gives the guests time to settle in before Sunday starts.'

'You're right.' Sister Joan put her share of the bill on the table. 'It would make more sense. Mother Dorothy left it to me to arrange dates so I'll let her know. Look, none of you has to come, you know.'

'We'd all like to come,' Barbara said firmly.

'I'm not sure if Colin can spare me,' Dodie said doubtfully.

'I'll bet he can!' Barbara spoke rallyingly. 'Take a few days out just for yourself. Joan, do you really have to go?'

'I think I'd better. Where are you going on to have dinner?'

'How about the National Theatre?' Derek suggested.

'We could see the play afterwards if there are any tickets available,' Barbara said. 'Wouldn't you like a trip to the theatre, Joan?'

The faint smell of dust and sweat, the creaking of the seats as they were tipped up or down, the hum of anticipatory conversation, the dimming of the lights—

'What I can do,' she said, squashing temptation, 'is call in

and see Serge if you like and tell him where you'll all be this
evening. He may have been held up and didn't manage to get
to the Abbey on time. It seems a shame he isn't here.'

'Flat Fifteen, Putney Walk,' Paul reminded her. 'He's
probably in the phone book.'

'I've time to go round,' Sister Joan said. 'I can get the
Underground from Tower Hill from here. I hope you'll all be
able to come down for the retreat. God bless!'

Walking away briskly she wondered if she'd meant that. The
reunion had been disappointing, but then probably most
reunions were. Had they all been in close sympathy they
would have kept in touch anyway. Perhaps there was a time
limit on certain relationships. The bickering she had just heard
had depressed her. Another week of it would be altogether too
much to stomach! She shook her head slightly at her own lack
of charity. People who were at peace with themselves and the
rest of the world weren't in need of a retreat!

Putney Walk, according to a map she consulted at the
bookstall, was near Victoria Station. She boarded the train and
sat, counting the stations again, hoping her sense of direction
would hold out. She had forgotten how tiring the city could be.
Had she ever swung along in jeans with a huge satchel at her
back, talking animatedly without even troubling to glance at
street signs?

It would have made sense to look up Serge Roskoff in the
directory but she wanted to see him personally. Serge had been
slight and blond, with Slavic cheekbones and a quick, light,
darting manner except when he was indulging in a mood of
Russian pessimism. She had liked Serge. It would be
interesting to find out if he too had changed, or hardened into
the personality that wasn't yet fully formed during their
student days.

Putney Walk was a broader street than she had expected,
with houses of decaying gentility down both sides of it and a
bookmaker's establishment on the corner.

With a spurt of annoyance she realized she didn't have the
house number, only the flat number, and none of the houses
seemed big enough to have fifteen flats.

After a moment she turned and went into the bookmaker's,
noting with relief that only a couple of customers lounged

against the counter.

'Excuse me, but would you have any idea where a Flat Fifteen might be?' she asked.

The man behind the wiremesh screen of the counter looked at her with pouched, empty eyes.

'Numbers ten, eleven and twelve have been turned into one building,' he said.

'So the number will be there? Thank you very much.' She went out, the other men still intent on the television screen beyond the wiremesh.

Number ten, eleven and twelve were in the centre of the left-hand row, the three front doors enlarged into one, bow windows bulging above with paint peeling from the frames. Sister Joan mounted the steps and looked at the list of namecards slotted into the spaces above the letterboxes in the lobby. Here it was! S. Roskoff. Flat 15. There was no sign of a bell to ring.

She checked the numbers on the ground floor and took one of two staircases that rose up out of the larger hall beyond. Whoever had done the conversions here hadn't had much respect for late Regency architecture. The staircases were original, their lines graceful but they were shored up with pinewood and heavily varnished and in the space where the centre staircase had been were a couple of wheeled bins.

She had picked the correct staircase anyway. Toiling up the stairs where damp stains mingled with erotic, ill-spelt advice to the passerby, she crossed landings from which doors bearing odd numbers opened or, in this case, remained shut, and went on climbing.

Light filtered through beautifully mullioned, grubby windows and under the soles of her feet the linoleum was cracked and roughened. Paul had mentioned something about an exhibition. Either it hadn't taken place or it had been a failure, she decided, because nobody with any money would live in a place like this. And Serge had had a sense of beauty that made him fastidious even as a student. She recalled his pained expression when he was offered coffee in a plastic cup or when one of the others came in with the wrong colour sweater on.

Number Fifteen was at the top of the building, its door barring her way. She lifted her hand to knock and stopped as she saw the door was slightly ajar already.

'Sèrge? Serge!'

Pushing the door wider she rapped on it anyway.

The apartment behind the door was two or three rooms knocked into one, a huge skylight in the sloping roof in addition to the large picture window at one end. It was easy to see that Serge had rented this place because, whatever its other defects, it made a perfect studio. She went in and let the door swing closed behind her.

The floor was dusty, bare of rugs, though a heavy tapestry hung against one wall. Out of a dark jungle, redolent with greens and browns and the yellow of corruption, golden eyes slanted with the vague shapes of animals to suggest rather than depict the waiting savagery. On the floor next to it a double bed was neatly made and covered with a soiled white duvet. There was an easel with no canvas on it, a tall cupboard, a couple of chairs and a dais with a stool and a potted plant on it.

'Serge?' Sister Joan stood in the middle of the space and heard her voice echo off the walls. 'Serge, are you here?'

There were two inner doors. She opened one and looked into a shower room with a toilet and wash basin. The other opened into a small kitchen with a large boiler taking up most of the space, a small but shiny cooker, dishes ranged neatly on wall shelves. The sink in the corner had a crack in it but the taps had been polished.

'Serge!' She crossed to the dais and sat down on the stool there, gazing about her in perplexity.

Serge certainly lived here. She recognized the little touches he would have added to the basic furnishings, the shine he'd given the taps and cooker. He'd liked to cook and he'd been fussy about hygiene, insisting that a meal should delight every sense apart from that of taste.

Serge surely wouldn't go out and leave the door unlocked. Not in London! Not in any town these days.

'What the hell are you doing here?'

The door had opened wide and a girl with bright ginger hair and a sharp, freckled face dominated by enormous and beautiful green eyes stood there, a shawl trailing from her thin shoulders and only half concealing garments that looked as if they were rejects from a thrift shop.

'My name's Sister Joan. I'm waiting for Serge Roskoff,' Sister Joan said, rising. 'The door was unlocked – ajar in fact so I came in.'

'Lock's broken. Been broken for ages,' the girl said, crossing to a table and dumping a couple of plastic carrier bags on it. 'What did you want?'

'I came to see Serge. Are you a friend of his?'

'I'm Tits,' the girl said. 'Short for Titania. My real name's Patricia but Serge said I was a Titania.'

'Are you a—?' Sister Joan hesitated. 'Are you a friend of his? He and I were in college together a long time ago.'

Before you were born probably, she added silently, and wondered uneasily if Serge had taken to cradle-snatching.

'At art college?' The green eyes were suddenly alert.

'A long time ago. Do you know when Serge will be back? Only I've got a train to catch.'

'Better catch it then,' the girl said.

'He's away?'

'Actually he's dead.' The word came out flatly, lay between them like something obscene dropped on the bare boards of the floor.

'Dead?' Sister Joan repeated the word blankly. In her own mouth it was no prettier. 'When? What happened?'

'Does it matter?' the girl asked.

'Yes, it matters.' Sister Joan stepped down from the dais. 'I used to be a fellow student of his twenty years ago at the college of art. Of course it matters. What happened?'

'I've seen you somewhere before,' the girl said abruptly. 'You weren't a nun back then, were you?'

'No. Patricia, what happened?'

'He died last month,' Patricia said.

'How?'

'Overdose, what else?' Patricia shrugged and began to unpack some bread and fruit.

'Of drugs? Serge took drugs?'

Twenty years before they'd all smoked a little pot from time to time, considering themselves decadent and daring. She didn't recall any of them trying anything stronger, but in twenty years people changed.

'No,' Patricia said. 'He didn't take anything, ever. Wouldn't

let me even start. Said it'd addle my brain faster than anything. No, he never smoked and he never shot up or sniffed. Not ever.'

'But he died of a drug overdose?'

'Crack,' Patricia said. 'You've probably never heard of it.'

'Crack cocaine. Yes, I have heard of it. He took that? I don't understand.'

'The coroner understood all right,' Patricia said coldly. 'Artist, foreigner, shacked up with his bird – stands to reason he'd be on something or other.'

'Didn't you tell them?'

'I don't stick my neck out unless I can't help it,' Patricia said. She sounded cross and tired.

'How did he take the crack? Injection? I'm not awfully well up in these matters.'

'You wouldn't be, would you?' A faint glint of humour crossed the thin young face. 'He took a massive dose in his wine. That was what they said anyway.'

'Would that kill somebody?'

'Fast when it's mixed up with LSD and other stuff. It was a – a lethal cocktail, the coroner said.'

'You went to the inquest?'

'I sat at the back. Never let on that I knew him. The old girl downstairs came up to cadge some money for the gas meter and found him. Took her all of a shiver she said. Silly old bat!'

'What was the verdict?' Sister Joan asked numbly.

'Suicide,' Patricia said, beginning to stack the food on a shelf. 'He was an artist and his work wasn't selling well – hell, it wasn't selling at all! So it was natural he'd top himself, wasn't it? – they said.'

'Is that what you think?' Sister Joan asked.

'Doesn't matter what I think,' Patricia said viciously. 'I didn't even live here then. Moved in a couple of weeks ago. He'd paid up front three months in advance, same as he always did and the lock was broken so I moved in.'

'The landlord didn't mind?'

'Nobody minds about anybody round here,' Patricia said.

'But Serge did?'

'Serge did. About me anyway. He asked me in for a meal one evening. I was sitting on the doorstep and he was just coming

in. He asked me to come up and share his meal. And afterwards he didn't want paying – if you know what I mean.'

'Yes,' Sister Joan said. 'Yes, I do know.'

'It was all voluntary,' the girl said, her voice tinged with pride. 'He was a lovely man, like a dancer but he painted. All swirls and colours going in and out and light sparkling behind the picture. It was ever so good. He was a lovely man.'

'Yes. Yes he was.'

'Are you sure I haven't seen you—?' The green eyes were narrowed and then widened again. 'Yes you are! In the photo! He had a photo sent here a few days before he died. It's still here somewhere. I sold most of his clothes and things, but I stuck the photo – in the cupboard! I knew it was somewhere safe.'

She tugged open a corner cupboard, rummaged through a pile of newspapers and brought out a square envelope.

'That's you, isn't it?' She pulled out the photograph. 'You when you were young.'

'Younger,' Sister Joan said wryly, taking the snapshot. 'Yes, we're all here. Did he tell you about it?'

'Said you were all in college together and that you planned to meet up. I didn't mean that you're old,' Patricia said earnestly, 'and you do look young anyway. It must be very peaceful being a nun.'

'Not always.' Sister Joan nodded towards the envelope. 'Was that posted in London?'

'From W.1. Serge said, "Someone went up in the world! I wonder which one". I laughed and told him you didn't have to live somewhere upmarket in order to post a letter from there! And he said he supposed not.'

'And this came before he died?' Sister Joan handed the photograph back.

'A few days before. He was looking forward to the reunion. Even said he'd take me along but I told him not to be so silly. I don't know anything about painting.'

'What happened to his paintings?'

'There weren't many here,' Patricia said, quickly and defensively. 'He told me that when he was an old, old man he was going to leave everything to me anyway because his family was all in Russia and he'd never gone back even when the Cold

War ended. I sold three or four of them down Portobello Road. They were ones that he got ready for an exhibition but he was let down by the gallery at the last moment. I think he got let down a lot. Too trusting!'

It was not something of which the girl standing opposite her could be accused, Sister Joan thought. The sharp little face was streetwise, the eyes no longer innocent.

'Did he leave a letter?' she asked aloud. 'A suicide note?'

'Not unless the old girl downstairs found one and didn't hand it in,' Patricia said. 'Anyway I don't think he did do it himself. I think someone put the stuff in his drink as a joke or something.'

'Who?'

'Don't know. I wasn't here all the time,' Patricia said. 'Only now and then when I felt like it. He didn't only ask me up here. Dropouts Delight this place was.'

'But you were special?'

'Yes.' An indefinable sweetness had come into the hard little face. 'Yes, I was special to him. That's why he was going to leave me everything. He really meant that!'

'I'm sure he did,' Sister Joan said. 'Look, I have a train to catch. If you think of anything else here's my address and phone number. Or if you need help.'

'I'd not be likely to be coming to a convent for it,' Patricia said.

'No, of course not, but if anything did crop up – do you know what happened about the funeral?'

'He was cremated,' Patricia said. 'I think he had some insurance or something that paid for it. Anyway I didn't go.'

'And he was looking forward to the reunion?'

'Yes. At least—' Patricia hesitated. 'He said he was but he did go a bit quiet from time to time after he had the photo. Kept taking out the old newspapers and looking through them.'

'Newspapers?'

'This lot here.' Patricia went back to the cupboard and pulled out the pile. 'I was going to toss them out when I got round to it. He was quite neat really, clean, but he kept the papers.'

'May I have them – that's if you don't want them, of course?'

'Help yourself.' The girl's voice was indifferent again.

'Have you read them?' Sister Joan slid them carefully into one of the newly emptied carrier bags.

'I'm not one for reading,' Patricia said.

'Thank you. You will get in touch if you remember anything else? Serge was a friend of mine.'

'Serge was everybody's friend,' she said bitterly. 'I reckon he died of that! Now if you don't mind I've my own life to lead.'

She was moving towards the little kitchen, eyes hard, lips tight. In a moment she was likely to burst into tears and anyone who witnessed that would never be forgiven.

'God bless,' Sister Joan said, and went out and down the stairs rapidly. At the end of the street was an unvandalized phone booth. She checked the directory at the side and rang the restaurant at the National, waiting for several minutes until Barbara's voice sounded at the other end.

'Yes?'

'It's Sister Joan. I haven't many coins left. Serge died a month ago.'

'What! Another one!' Barbara's voice had risen.

'An overdose apparently. I have to go now. Ring me?'

'Yes, of—'

The line went dead. Sister Joan replaced the receiver and picked up the carrier bag.

Serge was dead. The phrase kept pace with her as she walked towards the station. Serge had been life-loving, full of life. It seemed wrong, out of true, like a picture drawn out of perspective to imagine him dead by his own hand.

'Life,' Serge had said, 'is a gift, my friends!'

From his lips it hadn't sounded like a cliche.

She wondered suddenly as she walked what the odds were against three members of one particular group all dying violently before they were forty.

Four

'So what did you have to eat?' Sister Gabrielle asked, hitching herself higher in her chair.

'Smoked salmon sandwiches, a glass of white wine and coffee,' Sister Joan said.

'With cream I hope? No sense in spoiling yourself if you don't do it thoroughly!'

'Black coffee,' Sister Joan said, smiling faintly. 'Giddy young things like me must set limits you know!'

'I had smoked salmon once,' Sister Mary Concepta said wistfully from her own chair in the infirmary. 'It was delicious.'

'And London was still London, I suppose?' Sister Gabrielle was looking at her enquiringly.

'Most crowded,' Sister Joan said.

'And you saw your old friends. That must've been lovely,' Sister Mary Concepta said.

'Yes.'

'I could do with some exercise.' Sister Gabrielle heaved herself to her feet. 'Have you time to take a turn in the garden?'

'Yes, of course, Sister. Shall I get your cloak?' Sister Joan hastened to help.

'Don't fuss, girl. The day's warm enough. Come along!'

'Sister Mary Concepta—?' Sister Joan looked over at the other old lady and saw she had fallen into a doze.

'Mary Concepta can't keep awake for longer than a couple of hours these days,' Sister Gabrielle disapproved. 'You'd never think she was only eighty-one, would you? Why, I can give her five years and still stay conscious for most of the day.'

'You're a marvel, Sister,' Sister Joan assured her.

'I hope so.' Sister Gabrielle had reached the back door and

thrust it open with her stick. 'Better let me have your arm here. These cobbles are very picturesque but tricky for ageing feet.'

With the old lady leaning on her arm Sister Joan traversed the yard, passed beneath the arch into the walled gardens of the cloister.

'We'll sit under the mulberry tree for a few minutes,' Sister Gabrielle said.

'Yes, of course, Sister.'

Seated on the stone bench, Sister Gabrielle reached up to pat the gnarled trunk of the heavily laden tree.

'This tree was a mere stripling when I was a postulant,' she said. 'I was nineteen then. Not in this order, of course. Mary Concepta and I came over from the Sisters of Charity so that the new order could have a core of trained religious when it was first approved. But we had a mulberry tree in my own old mother house and when I saw this one I felt at home.'

'I never thought of that before,' Sister Joan said. 'Of many of the older nuns transferring from other orders.'

'Oh, it was quite voluntary,' Sister Gabrielle said. 'Not nearly as difficult a transition as coming in from the outside world must have been. What's troubling you, Sister? You've had a shadow in your eyes since you got back yesterday. You're not regretting coming into the religious life, are you? After meeting your friends again?'

'No, of course not!' Sister Joan exclaimed. 'Rather the contrary in fact. I was glad to get back here.'

'Then what's the trouble?' Sister Gabrielle demanded.

Sister Joan suppressed a grin. No ladylike hinting for Sister Gabrielle. She came straight to the point.

'You know I went to a reunion with my old classmates from the college of art?' she began.

'Mother Dorothy told us. A neat way of drumming up business for the retreats and having a day off yourself. What went wrong?'

'There were ten of us due to meet in Westminster Abbey,' Sister Joan said. 'Seven of us were there.'

'A fairly good proportion I would have thought. People are always planning reunions and then forgetting all about them when the allotted day arrives.'

'The other three didn't turn up because they were dead.'

'All about your own age?'

She nodded.

'Well, people still die young unfortunately,' the older nun remarked. 'We like to pretend it doesn't happen.'

'Two accidents and a supposed suicide?'

'Supposed?' Sister Gabrielle patted the bench beside her. 'Sit down and tell me about it, girl.'

'Sally Mount married Derek Smith, one of our class too,' Sister Joan said slowly. 'I hadn't heard they were married. Derek is fairly successful as an artist but I got the impression his sales have been falling off recently. Maybe people just aren't investing in paintings these days. Apparently they'd been married for fourteen years very happily and then two years ago Sally fell out of the top storey of a multistorey car-park in the city. You know the kind of place I mean?'

'By description only I'm glad to say,' Sister Gabrielle said. 'I've never been in a multistorey monstrosity in my life! Were there children?'

'No. Derek said not.'

'He was there yesterday?'

'Yes. He was genuinely upset about Sally. That was obvious. Not still grieving beyond reason, of course, but sad about what had happened. Sally had largely given up her own work in order to deal with Derek's affairs and I gained the impression that she'd been invaluable.'

'Can someone accidentally fall out of a car-park, or was that the suicide?'

'Apparently the multistorey block was badly designed and there'd already been some complaints. Anyway she stepped round a guard board and leaned out and fell.'

'And the others?'

'Bryan Grimes – he illustrated children's books – he came from Lincolnshire and had gone back there to live. He was killed by a hit-and-run driver last year. Serena had seen it in a newspaper or something – or perhaps it was Dodie. I can't recall.'

'Serena and Dodie,' Sister Gabrielle repeated. 'What peculiar names some parents choose for their offspring!'

'Serena is the daughter of the Clark biscuits people, terribly rich and plump and always marrying the wrong man and rather sweet underneath it all,' Sister Joan said. 'Dodie illustrates Christmas cards when she's not being a wife and mother. She's small and respectable and rather smug. Then there was Barbara Ford there. She's been living in New Zealand for years and she gave up art years ago and went into public relations. She was always terribly quiet and dull but she's blossomed out, smartened up – it was difficult to recognize her. Fiona and Paul were there too out of the original bunch.'

'A married couple?'

'Hardly!' Sister Joan's lips quirked. 'Paul's affections don't tend that way. He designs things for television and is terribly flip and camp.'

'Sister, please speak English!' Sister Gabrielle chided.

'Sorry, Sister. He's rather shallow and effeminate in a very obvious way. Fiona is very beautiful, still very beautiful I mean. She was always stunning. She never married which surprised us all, I think, and she teaches art these days.'

'And the supposed suicide?'

'Serge Roskoff.' Sister Joan's voice had softened perceptibly. 'He was Russian, rather beautiful in a brooding Slavic way, and very talented. Everybody liked Serge. He was a kind person, truly kind. Anyway he wasn't there and as I had to leave early I went round to his flat to remind him about the reunion.'

'And?'

'He was found dead of a drug overdose last month,' Sister Joan said. 'I met a – girl, a friend of his who'd moved into his flat after he died. She said he never took drugs.'

'Then wouldn't he be more likely to use them as a means of suicide?' Sister Gabrielle said.

'He wasn't the sort to commit suicide, Sister. He cared too much about other people's feelings, loved life too much. He hadn't even left a note. It was out of character.'

'You hadn't seen him for nearly twenty years. He might have changed.'

'From what the girl, Patricia, told me he hadn't changed at all. Anyway that's what bothers me.'

'Mother Dorothy mentioned a photograph.'

'We were all sent a copy of a group snapshot we had taken during our first term. That was when we arranged our reunion in twenty years' time. I'd almost forgotten all about it. I certainly haven't got the original photo any longer.'

'Who'd sent the photo?' Sister Gabrielle enquired.

'Nobody who was at the reunion yesterday and Sally and Bryan have both been dead for more than a year. I thought it might have been Serge but Patricia showed me a copy of the photograph that he'd received. All posted in London.'

'There's probably a reasonable explanation for all of it,' Sister Gabrielle said. 'Coincidences do happen, you know. So why not put it out of your mind and concentrate on something more worthwhile?'

'You're probably right.' Sister Joan rose. 'I have to get on with the preparations for our first retreat. I've got to persuade Mother Dorothy that we'd better lay out a little capital on new mattresses. Visitors won't appreciate ours.'

'Excellent for the spine,' Sister Gabrielle said, allowing herself to be hauled to her feet. 'Have we any bookings yet?'

'Not yet. I did mention it to the others at the reunion,' Sister Joan said, 'but that was before I heard about – anyway, I'm beginning to wish I'd kept quiet. I know we need visitors but the truth is that – they're all part of my past but I moved on years ago.'

'Friends become acquaintances again?'

'They were never really close friends,' she said. 'Barbara left during our second term to nurse her sick father and never came back. The rest of us didn't really keep in touch at all. I ran into Dodie once years ago and Paul says he tried to contact Serge about six months ago with a view to getting him some publicity on television for an exhibition he was holding but he never got any reply and Patricia said there hadn't been an exhibition after all. We weren't bound by any tie of loyalty or fidelity or even mutual liking.'

'They probably won't come down anyway,' Sister Gabrielle said, giving the mulberry tree a final pat. 'I'd better let you get on with your work, Sister. I shall go and say a prayer in chapel for the souls of the faithful departed. For you too.'

'Thank you, Sister.'

'Oh, praying is about all the good I can do these days,' Sister Gabrielle said cheerfully. 'Well, that's why we're all here!'

They walked at Sister Gabrielle's pace round to the front of the main building. The rough grass stretched before it to the open gates and beyond the gates the moor had an autumnal glow. The old lady paused to look at the view.

'I always liked spring best,' she observed. 'That's something we can start to look forward to as soon as Christmas is over!'

It was her way of saying that life went on, Sister Joan supposed, turning to mount the shallow steps to the front door which stood hospitably open. Alice lay in a patch of sunlight, pretending to be a trained guard dog.

'The rest I can manage,' Sister Gabrielle said, shaking her younger companion off like an irritating fly. 'Go and get on with your work. What comes will come. No sense in worrying about it beforehand!'

Sister Joan nodded and followed the other down the chapel corridor past the two small parlours with their dividing grille where lay visitors came into the chapel itself. Sister Gabrielle settled herself in her accustomed place, crossing herself as she fixed her attention on the altar and Sister Joan mounted the twisting stairs at the side of the small Lady Altar with its plaster statue and vase of late roses.

Over this wing stretched library and storerooms, the latter now adapted to provide two cells for Sister Hilaria and Bernadette. It had taken considerable ingenuity to get a couple of beds up here and to erect hardboard screens to divide up the space. Since the upper floor was blocked off from the sleeping quarters and dining-room on the upper floor and the one staircase was very narrow they had ended up by passing nearly everything through the windows. The result was surprisingly good, she decided, affording privacy to the novice mistress and her postulant without trespassing on the main library. On the other hand the remaining storeroom was now piled with boxes and clutter.

She had put the plastic bag with its sheaf of newspapers here, between two piles of old packing cases with a space where it was possible to crouch, reading by the light that came from a narrow skylight above.

There were about a dozen newspapers, some of them tattered at the edges. Glancing at the dates she noticed they were in chronological order, the earliest dated about ten years before. No items had been ringed round with pencil and nothing had been cut out. Sister Joan grimaced and started skimming the various paragraphs. Folding the newspaper, setting it aside, picking up the next which was from 1987, reading that one with the same rapidity, she could feel exasperation rising in her. There was absolutely nothing in the newspapers that related to the art college or the subsequent careers of its students. A filmstar had just eloped with a fifth husband; a child had been found strangled and a man arrested; there was an outbreak of typhoid fever in some obscure African state; a boy was missing and his parents were appealing for news; Parliament was going into recess. Even the personal columns yielded nothing of immediate interest.

She flicked more rapidly through the rest of the pile. There was a review of a television programme with considerable praise being lavished on the set design by Paul Vance. At least one familiar name had turned up! And Serge had kept the pile carefully which surely meant they'd all be important. In a more recent edition she found a brief paragraph about Sally's death. It was headed CAR-PARK TRAGEDY, and told her nothing she hadn't already heard. The last in the pile had a short report of an exhibition to be held in a gallery she'd never heard of, and written down the side of it, in pen, a list of numbers – dates, she guessed, looking at them more closely. They meant nothing but whoever had penned them had spanned nearly twenty years. One or two had question marks beside them.

It would take hours to go through every one of them, and she didn't have hours to spare. She put the newspapers back, rose, dusting down her skirt, and descended into the chapel again. Sister Gabrielle was right. Time passed and what would be would be. There wasn't the smallest excuse for her to go ferreting about in what certainly didn't concern her. At least, not yet!

She knelt briefly, noticing that Sister Gabrielle was still immersed in her devotions, and went back into the main part of the house.

'Sister, if you've nothing else to do can you drive into town for me?' Sister Teresa asked, coming from the kitchen.

'Yes, of course, Sister. What do you need?'

'I made out a list. Mother Dorothy thinks we ought to get extra flour and sugar and butter ready for any visitors who come for the retreat,' Sister Teresa said. 'I'd get them myself but

Sister Marie and I started turning out the cupboards and if we leave them half done—'

'I'll go right now,' Sister Joan said. 'Has Mother given permission?'

'She says it's all right to ask you, Sister.'

'Right then.' Sister Joan put her thoughts on hold, took the list and the money she had been given, and went out to the van which had replaced the ancient car.

She had painted the van with a charming design in pink and white which had practically sent Mother Dorothy into an apoplexy and had been hastily repainted a nice respectable, dull grey. Nevertheless the extra labour had been worth it, Sister Joan thought, with an inward grin as she settled herself behind the driving wheel and fastened her seatbelt.

One day they would probably build a tarmac road across the moor but she hoped it wouldn't be in her time. The track was wide, meandering over the browning heather in a lazily casual way that gave one leisure to enjoy the drive instead of hurtling from one place to the next with the scenery ignored as it flashed past the windows.

Brother Cuthbert was chopping wood at the side of the little schoolhouse which he was now occupying for a year while he was on sabbatical from his Scottish monastery.

Sister Joan drew to a stop as he looked up and waved, his bright red hair a flaming halo round his tonsure. His freckled, youthful face beamed at her window.

'Good morning, Sister Joan! Isn't it a glorious day? Were you in need of anything?'

'A bit of your cheerfulness,' she said wryly. 'Doesn't anything ever get you down?'

'Oh, from time to time,' he admitted. 'That's the beauty of the religious life, don't you find? Whenever something happens to depress you there's an instant remedy. And isn't it a privilege to be able to spend so much time praying for people who haven't got the time to pray for themselves?'

'Yes, of course!' Sister Joan felt a stab of shame. 'The truth is that I spent the day in London yesterday and it put me out of humour.'

'There are sad things happen in cities,' he agreed. 'Father Malone was telling me after mass this morning that he'd had a quick glance at the early edition of the paper and wished that he hadn't. Slander about the Royal Family, war in Bosnia, a dreadful murder in London.'

'What?' Sister Joan looked at him sharply. 'When?'

'Last night sometime. A young girl had her throat cut. She was found in the street. Father Malone said it reminded him of tales he'd read about Jack the Ripper. He asked me to pray in particular for the poor soul. Patricia – I don't think he told me the last name. Oh, I oughtn't to have mentioned it! You've gone white as a sheet!'

'I'm all right,' Sister Joan said with an effort. 'As you say cities are sad places. I'm going into town for some shopping. Do you need anything?'

'Not a thing in the world. Are you sure you're all right? I ought to think before I speak! Well, the poor little soul will be safe in heaven now, so that's a comfort.'

And her killer will still be walking about the streets, Sister Joan thought numbly as she switched on the ignition again and drove away.

There must be hundreds of girls in London named Patricia. There was no reason to suppose – there was every reason to suppose! In Sister Joan's experience life fell into a series of patterns and once the pattern had begun to be woven on the tapestry every thread connected it. Even the most seemingly inconsequential remarks and incidents had their place in the overall design.

She parked the van at the back of the small supermarket, conscientiously purchased all the groceries and lugged them into the vehicle, locked the doors and went at a brisk pace up the road to buy a newspaper and turn into the small café where it was possible to drink a cup of coffee without being deafened by loud music.

She half feared that the later edition wouldn't carry the story, but there was a paragraph on page three, headed PUTNEY WALK MURDER.

It was the same Patricia then. Sister Joan nerved herself to read the account, but it gave only the bare facts. At 1 a.m. the previous night the body of a girl had been found lying outside the closed premises of a betting shop at the corner of Putney Walk. The girl's throat had been cut but there were no signs of a struggle nor, as far as was known, any sexual connotation. The girl had been identified as Patricia Mayne, of no fixed address, aged eighteen. Police were conducting house-to-house enquiries.

Sister Joan folded the newspaper, paid for her coffee, and headed for the police station.

'Good morning, Sister Joan.' Constable Petrie, who was on desk duty, greeted her amiably. 'Nothing wrong up at the convent I hope?'

'We're all fine there,' she assured him, 'but I have some information which may be of help regarding the murder in Putney Walk. You've read about it?'

'Glanced at the paper this morning,' Constable Petrie said. 'Not on our patch.'

'I believe I was with Patricia Mayne shortly before she was killed,' Sister Joan said.

'You'd better see the boss,' Constable Petrie said. 'He's in his office.' He moved to tap at the half-glassed door and pop in his head to announce, 'Sister Joan's here, sir. Shall I send her in?'

'Thank you, Constable.' Sister Joan went into the small office where the tall, dark detective sergeant rose to shake hands, his face betraying pleasure at the sight of her.

'Sit down, Sister. Good to see you. Not bad news, I hope?'

'Good morning, Detective Sergeant Mill.' Seating herself primly, Sister Joan held out the folded newspaper. 'Perhaps you've seen this?'

'Earlier. It's not in our area so—?'

'Yesterday I went to London to a reunion of some old friends from art college,' she said. 'I met Patricia Mayne. There's no photograph of her but I'm positive it's the same girl. The meeting was in Putney Walk.'

'You'd better tell me about it.' He leaned both elbows on the flat-topped desk and gave her his full attention.

'A group of us met at Westminster Abbey and had lunch at the Tower,' she began.

'You believe in taking your pleasures sadly,' he said, with a twitch of a dark eyebrow.

'There were seven of us there out of a possible ten.' She bit her lip to stifle a laugh. 'Two had died and Serge Roskoff hadn't turned up. One of the others knew where he lived and as I had to get back early I offered to call round and see if he'd simply forgotten.'

'Serge Roskoff.' Detective Sergeant Mill wrote down the name, frowned at it and said abruptly, 'Russian. Avant-garde stuff, very symbolic. Never made the name for himself that was expected.'

'I didn't know you were interested in art!' she exclaimed.

'Only since I met you, Sister.'

'Oh. Well, anyway I went round to Flat Fifteen, Putney Walk but Serge wasn't there. The door was open so I went in. A moment or two later a young girl arrived. She said she was a friend of Serge's, that he'd christened her Titania but her real name was Patricia. She told me he'd committed suicide last month. An overdose.'

'I'm sorry.'

'He was a lovely person,' she said. 'One of the nicest of the bunch. Anyway the girl told me that he'd befriended her, taken care of her—'

'Slept with her?'

'She said it was voluntary,' Sister Joan said. 'I'm sure it was. Serge was a most attractive young man when I knew him. She'd moved into the flat because his rent was paid three months in advance and she'd nowhere else to go.'

'She wasn't living with him before?'

'Apparently not. She came and went, no strings. Anyway she told me that she didn't believe Serge had killed himself.'

'Accident?' He glanced up from the paper on which he was still making notes.

'She told me that Serge didn't do drugs. Certainly he never did when I knew him. He loved life – loved people. Oh, he could be a bit moody at times, but never deeply depressed. I found it hard to believe that he'd committed suicide too.'

'People can act out of character.'

'Yes, I know. Anyway I had a train to catch so I went away and came home.'

'At what time were you at the flat?'

'I got there just after five, stayed about – at the most fifteen minutes and then caught my train back to Cornwall.'

'Leaving Patricia Mayne in the flat?'

'Unpacking some groceries,' Sister Joan nodded. 'The point

is that my fingerprints will certainly be in the flat and when her connection with Serge is known they'll want to have my prints for elimination purposes, won't they?'

'Would you be willing to make a formal statement and give us a set of your prints?' Detective Sergeant Mill asked. 'I'll get in touch with the Metropolitan Branch and have a word with an old mate of mine there. That way we needn't have the place cluttered up with police officers.'

'May I ring the convent to tell them I'll be late for lunch?'

'Help yourself.' He indicated the telephone. 'I'll go and get the fingerprint squad alerted.'

Meaning he'd haul Constable Petrie from behind the front desk, Sister Joan thought, lifting the receiver.

'I'll tell Mother Dorothy you're delayed,' Sister Teresa said cheerfully on the other end of the line. 'Is everything all right, Sister?'

'Everything's fine. I'll be back as quickly as I can.'

Replacing the receiver, following Detective Sergeant Mill down to the room where the fingerprints of suspected persons were taken she felt thankful that she wasn't of their fraternity. The police station might be small and undermanned but justice still balanced her scales here.

'I've had a word.' Detective Sergeant Mill reappeared just as she was wiping her fingers. 'They'll be happy to accept a statement and your prints which will, of course, be destroyed immediately they've been eliminated from the inquiry. Actually you did right to come in straightaway. The fellow who runs the betting shop remembers a nun coming in to ask for directions just before five.'

'Was there any further information?' She paced beside him up the stairs.

'She was killed round about midnight. Taken from behind and her throat cut. A sharp old-fashioned razor apparently.'

'Nobody saw anything?'

'Apparently Putney Walk is a fairly quiet area,' he said. 'A few cruising cars, the occasional drunk, nothing very dramatic. People live separate lives, enclosed in their own private spaces. The owner of the betting shop had been out in the back, totting up the takings in a built-on office, and came through the front when he'd finished to lock up. He found her on the step.'

'The newspaper says she was found at about one o'clock in the morning,' Sister Joan said. 'Isn't that late to be totting up the accounts?'

'Apparently he does the accounting at different times and on different days, so that no would-be thief can discern any regular pattern. He's a respectable fellow. No form at all. Runs an honest business and only knew the girl by sight.'

'You'll fax my statement through?'

'As soon as you've made it. Just stick to the bare facts,' he advised.

'And not mention Patricia Mayne's suspicions?'

'Which were exactly?'

'She thought that someone doped Serge's drink for a rather unpleasant joke. He was apparently in the habit of inviting people up for a drink or a bit of supper.'

'Rather foolish in this day and age,' Detective Sergeant Mill commented. 'You can put that in if you like. It might have some bearing. Shall we start?'

He held the door of the office open.

Twenty minutes later she signed the statement and looked at him enquiringly. 'Is that all?'

'That's it. You've done your duty as a good citizen. Did you drive the van in?'

'To buy extra groceries for all the visitors we're hoping will book for one of our retreats.'

'Was that why Mother Dorothy gave you permission to attend the reunion?' he asked. 'To publicize the latest moneymaking venture of the Daughters of Compassion?'

'I suspect that was part of the reason,' she admitted.

'Did you get any bookings?'

'I told them about it, but I don't think it likely anyone will turn up.'

'You said seven of you were there?'

'Yes. Serge was absent. We didn't know then he'd died. Two others had died already.'

'Recently?' He was doodling idly on a pad.

'Sally – she married Derek Smith who was another of the group – died accidentally a couple of years back.'

'How?'

'She fell out of a multistorey car-park.'

'I didn't know you could,' he said.

'Apparently the design of the structure was faulty and there'd been complaints but she leaned out to look at the view before the extra safety precautions were fully implemented.'

'And the other?'

'Bryan Grimes was killed last year by a hit-and-run driver up in Lincolnshire,' Sister Joan said reluctantly.

'Oh?' He looked at her with more attention.

'It was an accident I'm sure,' Sister Joan said. 'The driver ought to have stopped, of course, but he panicked and drove on.'

'Nobody was charged?'

She shook her head.

'How about those who did turn up?' he asked.

'They can't possibly have had anything to do with Patricia Mayne's death!'

'I'm sure you're right,' he agreed. 'No, I'm interested in the sort of friends you made in college.'

'Friends is a bit of an exaggeration,' Sister Joan said. 'We never really bothered to stay in touch. I think it's like that often when you're young. When you're very young you imagine you'll keep the same friends for ever and you don't realize that life moves on.'

'I know Serge Roskoff kept up his painting. What about the others?'

'Sally married Derek Smith and devoted herself to his career. He used to sell quite a lot – mainly portraits, if I remember rightly. He runs a fine arts shop now. I don't know where. Bryan illustrated children's books.'

'And the others?'

'Dodie's married with two children. She paints cards for Christmas and birthdays. Barbara went into public relations – she never finished the college course. Serena Clark—'

'The biscuit people?'

'Yes. She got into college because her father made a huge donation to them. I'm not being spiteful. She was always honest about it, amused even. Anyway she didn't pass any of the examinations and since then she's been busy getting married and divorced. Paul Vance – but you'll have seen his work on television.'

'Vance was a compatriot of yours?'

'He's rather grand and precious now,' Sister Joan said with a faint grimace. 'Then there's Fiona. She teaches art part-time but her real talent is being beautiful. She was always stunning and also very sweet – a bit vague and fey.'

'And none of them knew Patricia Mayne?'

'I'm sure they didn't.'

'And none of you had kept in touch?'

'Oh, we occasionally ran into one another over the years, but that was all. We'd all grown up and moved on. Detective Sergeant, I really ought to get back!'

'Of course, Sister.' He rose at once, holding open the door. 'Give my regards to the community.'

'I will. Thank you, Detective Sergeant Mill. Constable Petrie.'

Hurrying back to the van she breathed a sigh of relief. She'd done her duty as a citizen, and could put it out of her mind. There'd been no point in mentioning the pile of old newspapers she'd brought away from the flat. They probably had nothing to do with anything anyway. She decided that she wouldn't waste any more time in scrutinizing them.

Driving back she reminded herself that at general confession she must remember she'd bought a cup of coffee without permission. It was annoying that after eight years in the religious life she still committed stupid little sins that blotted her copy book without giving her the chance to make some grand reformation.

Sister Marie was waiting for her at the gate, waving her scarf.

'What is it, Sister?' She drew to a halt and wound down the window.

'Good news!' Sister Marie's round face was beaming. 'While you were out a lady telephoned and made a block booking for our first retreat! She said six will be coming. All your old friends you met in London! Mother Dorothy is delighted!'

Starting up the van again, driving round to the back yard, Sister Joan wished she could share her superior's delight.

Five

'Yes, Sister?' Mother Dorothy looked expectantly at Sister Joan as the latter rose from her knees. 'You've heard the good news?'

'About the visitors? Yes, Mother Dorothy. On the face of it it's a splendid start.'

'On the face of it?' The prioress pushed her steel-framed spectacles higher on her small nose and gestured to the stool by her desk. 'Sit down and explain that remark.'

'This morning I heard that a young girl called Patricia Mayne had been murdered in London,' Sister Joan said, seating herself. 'She was found around one o'clock this morning in Putney Walk with her throat cut. The point is that I met the girl myself several hours earlier.'

'Oh?' Mother Dorothy rested her chin on her hand and waited.

'Ten of us were supposed to meet at Westminster Abbey as I told you,' Sister Joan said. 'Seven of us actually turned up and went along to the Tower for lunch. I told you that.'

'And that two of your old group had died and you volunteered to call in on the other missing member of your class only to be told that he, God rest his soul, had committed suicide last month. Yes?'

'The girl who told me about Serge Roskoff was Patricia Mayne,' Sister Joan said.

'I see.' Mother Dorothy nodded slowly. 'That was why you requested permission to be late for lunch. Obviously you had to report to the police.'

'I had my fingerprints taken for elimination purposes and made a statement that was faxed to the Metropolitan Branch.

Detective Sergeant Mill believes that will be the end of the matter as far as I'm concerned.'

'I wish I could be as optimistic as Detective Sergeant Mill,' Mother Dorothy said. 'In my experience you have the most unfortunate habit of getting mixed up in events that have nothing to do with your life as a religious. However I fail to see why the prospect of your other friends coming here for a week-long retreat should worry you.'

'Mother Dorothy, three of us are dead,' Sister Joan said earnestly. 'Sally was killed a couple of years ago. She leaned out of the upper floor of a multistorey car-park and fell, and last year Bryan Grimes was knocked down and killed by a hit-and-run driver, and now Serge is dead.'

'A sad sequence of events. I am sorry there was a gloom cast over the reunion.'

'Three deaths, each one unusual, in the space of two years among the same group of people. Reverend Mother, what's your opinion?'

'That you have a vivid imagination and a craving for variety,' Mother Dorothy said snubbingly. 'Neither do I accept your premise of there being anything extraordinary about these particular deaths. You told me that none of you bothered to keep in regular contact with any of the others once your college days were behind you. You were a collection of separate individuals, that's all, living separate lives. Accidents happen all the time.'

'Patricia Mayne's death wasn't an accident.'

'She was a neighbour of Serge Roskoff's?'

'A stray kitten he fed now and then as far as I could gather,' Sister Joan said. 'Serge was always like that, kind and generous. Patricia – the girl was eighteen, red-haired and superficially tough, probably on the game.'

'A soiled dove,' Mother Dorothy corrected severely.

'More like a soiled sparrow,' Sister Joan said. 'Streetwise and suspicious. She didn't believe Serge had been a suicide. He loved life and he didn't do drugs.'

'Another accident?'

'You can't take crack cocaine and LSD mixed up together by accident,' Sister Joan said. 'Patricia thought that someone might have given it to him as a joke, a sick joke that went wrong. But now Patricia herself is dead and she didn't cut her own throat.'

'Poor child!' Mother Dorothy blessed herself thoughtfully. 'I shall pray for her. Sister, do you have any reason to suppose that any of your other old friends is mixed up in this?'

'Not really.'

'Only your own instincts, is that it?' Mother Dorothy compressed her small mouth and looked as if she thought poorly of instincts. 'Meanwhile, thanks to your excellent publicity, six of your former fellow students are coming here for a week. There isn't anything very surprising about that. My advice to you is to concentrate on running the retreat in a fitting manner, making our guests as comfortable as possible, and leaving odd coincidences alone.'

'Yes, Mother Dorothy, but—'

'No buts, Sister!' Mother Dorothy rapped the desk sharply. 'You may go. Oh, the postulancy is looking very nice. You've all worked hard on it. We shall pray that this week is only the first of many. *Dominus vobiscum.*'

'*Et cum spiritu tuo.*' Sister Joan dipped her knee and departed, unsatisfied.

She bent her steps towards the postulancy, the old dower-house where widowed Tarquin ladies had once lived out their final years. It was at the other side of the tennis court, separated by a low wall from the grass-grown court with its rusted posts. She never went down the shallow steps without imagining how it must once have been, with the nets taut and young men in white flannels and girls in the loose skirts and long bodices of the twenties. The court hadn't been used for years despite her hints to Mother Dorothy who had countered her argument that the community needed exercise by pointing out reasonably enough that with vegetables, fruit and flowers to be tended, gravel walks to be weeded and raked, hedges clipped and Alice to train the necessity for a game of tennis came rather low on her list of priorities.

The postulancy was a simple, two-storey building, displaying the graceful Georgian proportions of the main house, though every trace of gold leaf had been removed and the walls whitewashed. The front door led into a narrow hall with stairs rising out of it, and the rooms subdivided at each side.

There was a lecture room with a row of chairs and a lectern, a library containing devotional works judged suitable for intending religious, and a much smaller room where the postulants had their own modest recreation. On the other side of the hall were a large room for meditation, a narrow parlour for the novice mistress, and a small kitchen. The library books had been carried up to the newly adapted storerooms, and replaced with a selection of paperbacks by middle of the road writers who could be guaranteed not to shock. There were four ashtrays in the recreation-room. Sister Joan trusted the hint not to light up anywhere else would be taken, and in Sister Hilaria's parlour a camp bed waited for herself.

'You had better sleep on the premises as you are to lead the retreat,' Mother Dorothy had said briskly.

Sister Joan sighed, wondering if leading a retreat was quite in her line, and went up the narrow stairs to the six cells above, each with its single bed, extra mattresses still wanting, its ewer and jug on the broad windowsill, its shelf for books and hooks behind a plastic cover for clothes. Since she was sleeping downstairs there was no reason for anybody to share. She took out the neatly printed slips of paper from her pocket and fixed them to the doors. Dodie, Barbara, Serena and Fiona on the left of the corridor, Paul Vance and Derek Smith on the right. The two small bathrooms at the end were functional and clean and that was about all that could be said for them. She fixed the signs Ladies and Gentlemen and went downstairs again.

There was the usual routine of the convent into and around which the visitors would be fitted. Private meditation in the chapel from 5.15 to 7 for those who wanted it – she doubted if any of them would! Low mass at 7, with breakfast at 8.

'Their breakfast can be prepared in the postulancy,' Mother Dorothy had said. 'Sister Marie will come over and help you. We must make it absolutely clear that the menu is vegetarian.'

Sister Joan doubted if a slice of dry bread, a piece of fruit and a cup of coffee would be considered adequate by paying guests. There would be fruit juice, cereal, buttered toast and eggs or tomatoes in addition.

The mornings were free with a list of local beauty spots to visit, details of buses though she guessed most people would come by car, and picnic lunches available or, if the weather broke, cold salad with fish or cheese in the postulancy. In the afternoon there would be a talk followed by a discussion group and a chance for the visitors to meet the professed nuns.

'Who knows but we may find another postulant?' Sister Hilaria had said, her eyes dreamy at the delightful prospect.

The evening meal would be taken with the community after which the visitors were free to amuse themselves, though Sister Teresa had suggested hopefully that they might enjoy joining in the community recreation.

'When there are only ladies present I see no difficulty,' Sister Perpetua had declared, 'but I think Reverend Mother will agree with me that we don't want men cluttering up the entire place.'

'Oh, for a bit of clutter!' Sister Gabrielle had said audibly, and Mother Dorothy's mouth had twitched.

'Now for the talks!' Sister Joan spoke aloud and jumped as someone tapped on the window pane.

'Detective Sergeant Mill!' She hastened to open the door. 'Has something happened?'

'Mother Dorothy said you were probably over in the postulancy. Is it all right to come in?'

'Yes, of course. Sit down. What's happened?' she demanded.

'I drove over to let you know that I did some phoning around after what you told me,' he said. 'The other deaths you mentioned – three from the same group within two years – struck me as unusual. Anyway I thought it worthwhile to check up.'

'Mother Dorothy would say you had a vivid imagination too,' she said wryly.

'Call it a hunch. Anyway this time my hunch was apparently way off course. Sarah Smith née Mount had been doing some late afternoon shopping in town, went back to her car just as lighting-up time arrived and must have ignored the warning board and gone over to look out of the aperture on the top floor. She leaned out, presumably to see the view better, overbalanced and fell. There was a witness.'

'Oh?' Sister Joan looked at him.

'A couple coming along the pavement opposite. One of them glanced up and saw her leaning out. He mentioned it to his wife, said it looked dangerous, and the next instant she fell. There was nobody else there at that moment. The couple rushed to her but she'd been killed instantly. They gave evidence at the inquest.'

'She was alone then? An accident.'

'A freak accident but they do occasionally happen. There had been complaints about the design and the building's more secure now.'

'And Bryan Grimes? Did you find out anything about him?'

'Unmarried, lived in Lincolnshire and made a good living illustrating books for children. In fact I think my own two have a couple of his. Anyway I got in touch with the Boston police and made a few enquiries. Bryan Grimes enjoyed walking it seems. Used to walk a few miles every evening. When he didn't come back from his walk his housekeeper assumed he'd put up for the night at a hotel; apparently he sometimes did that if he walked further than he intended. Some workmen found his body the next morning, multiple injuries caused by a speeding car. Nobody had seen anything and death must have been instantaneous. The case is still on file but it's doubtful it'll ever be solved. As for the Roskoff matter, there's nothing there either that doesn't suggest suicide. He lived alone, was inclined to be moody from time to time – a local doctor came forward and testified he'd been treating him for mild depression earlier this year.'

'No suicide note?'

'People don't always write one. It wasn't as if he had a family and needed to soften the blow by absolving them of guilt. The old lady who found him said that he often invited friends back to his studio for a drink or a bite of supper, but she couldn't recall anyone in particular. Oh, and Patricia Mayne didn't come forward at the inquest.'

'I think she avoids the authorities – avoided,' Sister Joan corrected herself. 'She was such a tough little girl that it's hard to believe she'd get herself killed.'

'Whoever did it certainly stepped out and cut her throat with one slashing cut. Right-handed and probably about six inches taller than she was.'

'And she didn't cry out?'

'Probably never had time. Whoever it was lowered her to the ground and walked off. Nobody saw, or heard a thing.'

'So that case is on file too.'

'And there seems to be no connection with any of the other deaths,' the detective sergeant said. 'No case.'

He sounded, she thought, ever so slightly disappointed.

'It was very nice of you to come over and tell me yourself,' she said, rising.

'You're getting the place ready for visitors?'

'Didn't Mother Dorothy tell you? The six who did turn up at the reunion made a block booking for the retreat.'

'You must have made a strong selling pitch,' he said.

'I didn't say very much at all,' she confessed. 'I felt a bit awkward about it, like peddling something they didn't want in the hope that they'd feel obliged to buy! Anyway they're all coming. I've been sorting out the accommodation. The next job I have is to arrange six talks for them to attend while they're here.'

'Talks on the religious life?'

'In a wide sense. Mother Dorothy has promised to give a talk on the history of the Order and Sister Perpetua is going to talk about ancient herbal remedies devised by the early monks, and I'm hoping Sister Gabrielle will talk about her life as a religious.'

'How about the morality of criminal detection?' he asked. 'Bringing in examples from Chesterton's Father Brown, Brother Cadfael, so on?'

'It sounds fun.' She beamed at him. 'You'll give the talk, of course?'

'I was thinking you'd be the right person. You've been involved in a few cases yourself so it wouldn't be too difficult.'

'I can think of nothing worse,' Sister Joan said frankly, 'than standing up in front of people and announcing myself as the nun who solves mysteries, or something equally ridiculous! And if one were to know the people personally – oh no!'

'I suppose I could spare an hour.' Detective Sergeant Mill frowned. 'I'd not mention your part in any of the cases of course, Sister. And it might give me a chance to take a look at your old friends.'

'Meaning your hunch wasn't so far out after all?' She looked at him sharply.

'Meaning nothing of the kind,' he retorted, smiling faintly. 'I'd be interested to find out the kind of people you used to hang out with, that's all.'

'We were fellow students back in 1974 for three years, except for Barbara Ford. Her father was very ill and she left college halfway through the second term to nurse him. Of the others – well Derek Smith married Sarah Mount quite a time after we all left. I didn't even know they'd been married let alone that Derek was a widower! We were never really that close any of us. I mean people think that artists ought to be friends simply because they're doing roughly the same thing but that doesn't always apply any more than it does to policemen.'

'Did anyone else marry anyone else?'

'No. Bryan and Serge were both single. Barbara isn't married and neither are Fiona or Paul Vance. Dodie married an engineer and Serena's on her second divorce.'

'Partnerships?'

'Nothing I knew about,' she said scrupulously.

'How many of them kept up their art?'

'Derek runs a fine arts shop as I told you: Paul's in television and Bryan was a children's books illustrator, and Dodie paints Christmas cards and Fiona teaches art part-time. She inherited some money from an aunt or someone recently and doesn't need to work full-time. You do think there's something odd about the deaths, don't you?'

'Nothing I can put my finger on. Walk back to the gates with me, Sister, will you? I left my car there and walked up to the convent. My way of getting some exercise.'

'I'll just lock up.' Suiting action to words, she put the postulancy key in her pocket and walked with him across the old tennis court.

'You said that none of you had kept in touch?' he said as they paced.

'Not all of us anyway. I told you all this when I came to the station. Why are you checking up?'

'Not because I don't trust your word,' he said, 'but I'm wondering why you haven't questioned the most obvious thing.'

'Which is?'

'If hardly any of you bothered to keep in touch why did seven of you turn up for the reunion twenty years later?'

'Oh, I'm sorry! It just didn't occur to me to – we all got a copy of a group photo that was taken of us sometime after we registered. Just a snapshot.'

'Who sent them round?' he asked.

'I don't know,' she said slowly, frowning in her turn. 'Nobody who was there at the Abbey had sent it. At least they all said they hadn't. We all decided that it must have been Serge since the photographs were sent out after Sally and Bryan died. But when I got to Serge's flat the girl, Patricia Mayne, showed me a copy of the same photo that he'd received. So it wasn't him either.'

'Where were they posted from?'

'All from W.1. I'm sorry but I merely assumed it was a reminder that the reunion was due.'

'Were there any messages with the photographs?'

'Not with the one I got, and the others said they hadn't had any either. The envelopes were printed I think, at least mine was.'

'May I see it?'

'It's here in my pocket. I'm afraid I threw the envelope away.'

'May I keep it for a day or two?' he asked.

'Yes, of course, but I don't see—'

'On second thoughts keep it yourself. ' He gave the photograph a searching look before handing it back. 'You haven't changed much, have you? What about the others? Did you recognize them at once?'

'Not Barbara Ford,' Sister Joan said. 'She was a shy, mousy creature in college. One of those repressed girls with an invalid father and too much responsibility, and her work was mediocre too. That sounds unkind but it's true. She worked very hard and yet it never looked quite right. She scraped through the examination at the end of our first term and then had to leave and didn't come back. Her father recovered and remarried and they all three emigrated to New Zealand. She's changed a lot! Now she's smart and vivid and very sure of herself and in public relations. Emigration did her a lot of good.'

'And the others?'

'They'd all developed in the way I'd have expected,' she said, climbing the steps between the high bushes. 'Derek always looked like a pirate and he looks now like the captain of pirates; Dodie is small and prim and I'm positive she has an Aga in the kitchen, and Fiona is lovely, perfectly lovely. I can't even scowl and say she'd obviously had a facelift because she obviously hasn't!'

'Serena Clark, Paul Vance?'

'Oh, Serena was always plump and vague and good-humoured. She's more so now, Paul – Paul is—' She hesitated.

'Paul is what?'

'Gay,' she said. 'I somehow never guessed that for a moment when we were at college but then twenty years back people weren't so open about these things. Now he's so effeminate and bitchy that I just couldn't credit it. I must have been green as grass when I was eighteen!'

'I think you were probably charming,' he said.

'Oh.' She felt her ready colour rising and managed a light laugh. 'Thank you, but it was a long time ago. We were all very young.'

'The point is,' he said, tactfully shifting the subject, 'that one of you must have sent copies of that photograph round and whoever did—'

'Had found out where we were all living?'

'Would that be very difficult?'

'I'm not sure. Paul Vance and Derek are fairly high profile so it wouldn't be very difficult to find out their whereabouts. Serena probably gets her picture in the gossip columns from time to time and Fiona's done quite a bit of modelling so she may still have an agent. Dodie's just a wife and mother – sorry, I didn't mean that to sound patronizing. The point is she's not a public person, though I suppose the publishers of her greetings cards could pass on mail for her – but I can't think how anyone knew I was in Cornwall. Most of them had heard that I'd entered the religious life but I hadn't contacted anybody.'

'Yet someone went to a lot of trouble to contact all of you and make sure you all met up on the appointed day,' Detective Sergeant Mill said.

'Simply to remind us of a reunion that most of us had half-forgotten about anyway? And if they did then why not say as much? It doesn't make much sense.' They had reached the front gates and she stopped, looking up at him with a troubled expression.

'I've no idea. The ploy was successful though, wasn't it?'

'Everybody who could did turn up, you mean?' Sister Joan nodded.

'And they're all coming to stay here.'

'Whoever sent the photograph round couldn't have known that,' she objected. 'This is a new scheme and there hadn't been any publicity.'

'Then someone seizes opportunities. Take care of yourself, Sister.'

'I will,' she promised. 'My regards to your – family.'

Three months previously Detective Sergeant Mill had been reconciled with his wife for the sake of their two sons. Sister Joan had never met them and had never enquired into his private life, so there was a faint hesitation in her question.

'Thank you.' He didn't enlarge on the subject but got into his car and backed out on to the track again.

'Sister! Sister!'

Luther was striding towards her, having apparently risen from a clump of bracken where, judging from the state of his garments, he'd slept. She stayed where she was, knowing that any sudden move on her part would send him rushing down the hill again. Luther was part gypsy, a cousin of sorts to Padraic Lee who lived in the Romany encampment and supplied the convent with fish. He was a tall, shambling fellow, vacant-eyed, with the bewilderment of a large child stamped on his irregular features.

'Sister Martha is needing help to pick the last of the apples and pears, Luther,' Sister Joan said, when he finally stood before her, shifting from one foot to another.

'I do well at the picking,' he assured her. 'Sister Martha gave me some apples and a mug of tea and a sweater for the cold nights.'

'Which you're not wearing, I see.'

"'Tis for best,' he said shyly. 'I'll be picking more just for the tea.'

'She'll be very pleased.' She had turned to go when his voice arrested her.

'Luther do have something for you, Sister,' he said.

'Oh?' She turned back to hold her hand out as she said coaxingly, 'May I have it then?'

'It came a week since,' he said, handing her the square envelope. 'I told the postman I'd bring it up straight.'

'But you didn't.'

'I forgot.' He hung his head, shuffling his feet. 'I didn't mean to be bad, Sister. It went in my pocket—'

'And clean out of your head. Thank you, Luther. Go and find Sister Martha and ask her what she needs.'

'Apples and pears, apples and pears!' he chanted softly as he loped past her.

She ought to take the envelope with its W.1 postmark and its printed address to Mother Dorothy who read all mail first, but after staring at the envelope with its bent and crumpled edges for a moment she pulled the flap open and drew out the snapshot.

The same group as before with no message or enclosure. Only the photograph was marked. The faces of Sally, Bryan and Serge had been obliterated by heavy black crosses and round her own smiling, youthful face a black circle had been drawn. Warning or threat, she wondered, as she shoved it deep into her pocket and walked back to the main building.

Six

'Your habit looks very dusty, Sister,' Sister Perpetua remarked, passing Sister Joan in the corridor. 'You ought to wear an apron when you're cleaning.'

'Yes, Sister.' Sister Joan met the older woman's irritable remark meekly, so meekly that the other shot her a suspicious look.

'It's not like you not to argue back,' she said. 'Are you feeling ill or have you decided to humour me because I'm getting old?'

'I'm humouring you,' Sister Joan said promptly. 'Anyway I haven't been cleaning. I've been rummaging about in the storeroom. I ought to have worn an apron though. One day we're going to have to find time to sort out all that stuff.'

'You sort it out! My hands are full,' Sister Perpetua said. 'The old ladies always seem to develop all varieties of aches and pains as autumn draws on. There was a time when I'd have coped with a smile instead of a snarl. I suppose the truth is that I'm dashing into the sere and yellow.'

'Don't look round,' Sister Joan warned. 'I'm treading on your heels.'

The brief conversation was cut short by the ringing of the bell summoning the nuns to chapel. A formal benediction was held on Wednesdays and Saturdays by either Father Malone or Father Stephens, but on other evenings there was a simple service of thanksgiving conducted by Mother Dorothy for a day well spent.

The trouble was that she didn't feel she'd spent the day particularly well. The morning had been occupied in carrying new mattresses across to the postulancy for the comfort of the intending guests, the afternoon in helping Sister David to tidy up the library, and when she had managed to slip away to take another look at the pile of old newspapers she'd brought away from Serge Roskoff's flat she'd found nothing in them of great interest. There were several reviews of Paul Vance's work, a brief item about Serena's first divorce, an advertisement for a book that Bryan Grimes had illustrated, but that only showed that from time to time Serge had kept newspapers in which his fellow students were mentioned. And the dates meant nothing, if they were dates at all and not something else entirely. She had wasted an hour, getting dusty, and not finding whatever it was she was supposed to be looking for.

Then there was the photograph that Luther had given her. Three crosses on people who were already dead, a circle around her own face. Meaning what? That she was next?

If anything does happen to me, she thought wryly, I shall be more annoyed at not knowing why it happened than at being dead!

'Tomorrow our visitors arrive,' Mother Dorothy was saying. 'Sister Joan will be leading the retreat.'

Too right! Sister Joan thought irreverently.

'Everything is in readiness for what we hope will be a pleasantly relaxing week for our guests away from the stress and strain of the outside world. Some of them may wish to converse with you, and it will be your responsibility to answer them with courtesy without allowing yourselves to be drawn into argument and, it goes without saying, without allowing these fleeting contacts with the laity to interfere with your spiritual duties. Sister Bernadette will not, of course, speak to anybody. There are to be some interesting talks given in my parlour during the week, and those of you whose duties permit are welcome to attend. I must warn you that two gentlemen are coming. You will not, of course, waste valuable time in long tête-à-têtes with them.' She paused, giving a dry little smile to demonstrate that she was joking.

'They are sleeping in the postulancy but will take their evening meal with us so that they get a flavour of convent life. While they are here the postulancy is out of bounds to everybody except Sister Joan, Sister Teresa and Sister Marie, who will be caring for the material wants of our visitors, and of course myself, though I can think of no reason why I should need to go over there. Are there any questions before we go to supper?'

'Are they coming by car?' Sister David asked. 'There's no garage.'

'I believe that was made clear.' Mother Dorothy consulted the paper in her hand. 'Mr Smith is driving down with Mrs Mason and Mr Vance. Miss Madox is also driving herself and bringing Mrs Clark with her. Miss Ford is coming by train. Sister Joan, you may take the van down and meet her. I'll give you the times later.'

'Yes, Reverend Mother.'

And why wasn't Barbara driving down? She bowed and resumed her place.

'Sister Joan, as our guests are arriving tomorrow,' Mother Dorothy was continuing, 'it would be best if you moved your things over to the postulancy during recreation, and then you can sleep over there tonight, settle in before the visitors arrive.'

'Yes, Mother Dorothy.'

'*Benedicite*.' The prioress turned to genuflect to the altar and went out, followed by the community in order.

'Won't you be a bit lonely over there all by yourself?' Sister Katherine whispered, tugging at Sister Joan's sleeve.

'I'll be fine,' Sister Joan whispered back. 'I'll take Alice with me.'

That decision was neatly overruled just as she'd collected her things after supper and was on her way down the stairs. At the foot of the gracefully carved balustrade Mother Dorothy stood, her expression one of calm approval.

'I know I speak for the whole community,' she said cordially, 'when I say that your agreeing to lead this retreat takes a great burden off our shoulders. Do you need help to carry anything?'

'No thank you, Mother. I haven't got much,' Sister Joan said.

'It's so convenient not to be weighed down with possessions. You'll lock yourself in after chapel? Since Alice is needed to guard the entire enclosure then we cannot spare her for just one person, though, of course, you haven't requested that.'

'Of course not,' Sister Joan echoed, wondering fleetingly if it was a grave sin to want to slap one's superior.

'I'll see you in chapel then.' Mother Dorothy mounted the stairs towards the recreation-room beyond the refectory where the rest of the community, save for Sister Hilaria and Sister Bernadette and the two lay sisters would occupy an hour in chatting, sewing, playing Scrabble and knitting.

There are so few of us, Sister Joan thought, lugging her holdall over the front threshold. The ideal number in a convent was nineteen, including prioress and novices. In medieval times there would have been troops of girls wishing to embrace a life that gave them security and a certain measure of independence. Nowadays that simply didn't apply. Girls went off to travel round the world or become secretaries, nurses, business tycoons, anything that they wanted, and fewer and fewer wanted the mystic marriage, the life of recollected prayer and duty.

It was darker than she had expected. She reminded herself to bring a torch when she came back later and started violently as a pair of headlamps scythed through the gloom.

'Running away, Sister? I knew you would sooner or later.'

Detective Sergeant Mill had alighted from the car and strode towards her.

'Only as far as the postulancy. Is something wrong, Detective Sergeant Mill?'

'Not as far as I know. Give me your bag and, for heaven's sake, call me Alan! The full title's a bit of a mouthful at the best of times.'

'Thank you – Alan. It's not very heavy.'

'What do you keep in it? Feathers?' He looked amused as he took the holdall.

'My smalls,' Sister Joan said mischievously.

'And why to the postulancy?'

'Our visitors arrive tomorrow so I'm sleeping over there tonight, settling myself in.'

'Where's Alice?'

'Probably having her supper. She's not my personal guard dog, you know.'

'I'm not interrupting the grand silence yet, am I?'

'Of course not. Even I wouldn't be chattering like this if we were in it.'

'Then I can tell you my findings.'

'Findings?' She looked at him sharply as they walked down the side of the main building but his face was shadowed.

'Knowing your habit of falling into criminal activities,' he began.

'You could've phrased that a bit better!' she exclaimed.

'Sorry, but you do have a habit of nosing out trouble! I've often been grateful that you're on the right side of the law,' he said. 'Anyway, I thought it as well to do a little preliminary research on your intending guests – just to be on the safe side. Nothing very detailed, I'm afraid. A matter of a few phone calls, that's all.'

'That was very considerate of you,' she said.

'On the contrary,' he returned, 'it's pure self-indulgence. The locals have been remarkably law-abiding recently. I have to show that I earn my salary or sit in my office twiddling my thumbs and hoping that somebody'll commit a crime! Anyway I made a few enquiries.'

'And?'

'Is it all right if I come into the postulancy for a few minutes? I made some notes.'

'There's no rule forbidding it,' Sister Joan said, forbearing to add that the idea that a sister might entertain a gentleman visitor there had probably never occurred to anyone!

They had reached the tennis court. Walking across it, the tall figure at her side, she wondered if she were putting herself into an occasion of sin. Surely not! She and Detective Sergeant Mill were occasional colleagues and unofficial ones at that. Perhaps it had been a mistake to agree to call him by his Christian name. It stripped away a barrier that had been protective for them both.

'Come into the lecture room.' She unlocked the front door and went ahead of him, switching on lights as she did so.

'This was the old dower-house, wasn't it?' He looked round at the bare, whitewashed walls, the plain wooden cross, the dais and semicircle of chairs, the table.

'Where they used to park mother-in-law when the bride arrived,' she nodded. 'Sit down, Detective – sorry, Alan. What have you found out?'

He opened his notebook, seating himself opposite her at the table.

'Let's go through your little group briefly,' he said. 'Dorothy Jones, born 1955, in London. Entered the college of art in 1974, graduated in 1977. Married Colin Mason, a civil engineer, in 1979. Two children. No criminal record. Earns some money, not much, by designing greetings cards. Anything to add?'

Sister Joan shook her head. 'Dodie was always neat and prim, full skirts and sweaters and pearl chokers.'

'Barbara Ford, born 1956. Manchester. Entered college in 1974, left in the spring of '75.'

'Her father was dangerously ill.'

'James Ford.' He referred to his notes again. 'He died in 1975.'

'What!' Sister Joan shot upright. 'There's some mistake there! Her father recovered, married a woman called Claire, and they all three went to New Zealand.'

'According to my information,' Detective Sergeant Mill said, 'her father was killed in a plane crash in July, 1975. He was a keen amateur pilot, and his glider came down during a storm. Barbara certainly went to New Zealand – in 1976. She returned to this country five years ago. Does PR work for a computer firm.'

He was looking at her enquiringly.

'She was always mousy and shy,' Sister Joan said. 'When I met her in London I didn't recognize her at all at first. She's blossomed out, become very elegant.'

'Sarah Mount,' he was continuing. 'Born Lincolnshire in 1956. Entered college in 1974. Married Derek Smith in 1978, a year after leaving college. They seem to have lived mainly in London. No children. She was killed in 1992, falling from a multistorey car-park. Two witnesses said she was alone. Verdict accident. The local council was censured for not safeguarding the car-park more efficiently. You know if her husband had decided to sue he'd probably have won substantial compensation.'

'Sally was a nice person,' Sister Joan said musingly. 'Not very talented but nice.'

'Serena Clark.' His mouth quirked in a smile. 'Very wealthy. Born 1956, in London. Entered college in 1974. Failed her graduation. I suppose daddy's money got her in in the first place. Married Rupert Hawstead in 1978, divorced in 1988. Married Seth Paget in 1990, now in the process of getting a divorce. Kept her maiden name. No children.'

'And then there's Fiona.'

'Fiona Madox.' He glanced at his notes again. 'Born in London in 1956. Graduated in 1977 from the college of art. Went to the States in 1979. Had a small role in some television soap and modelled – is that a euphemism?'

'No. She was a nice girl,' Sister Joan said.

'You're very faithful to your friends. Anyway she returned from the States in 1984. Worked as a professional model until 1987, then took a part-time job teaching art at a secondary school.'

'She inherited some money from an aunt so doesn't need to work full-time.'

'That's fresh information.' He made a note.

'And the men? Did you look into their histories too?' Despite her liking for him there was a shiver of distaste in her voice.

'Derek Smith, born 1954 in Cornwall.'

'Of course! I'd forgotten that!' she exclaimed. 'He looks like someone left over from the Armada.'

'Dark, piratical. Entered college in 1974, graduated in 1977. Made a good living as a commercial artist – portraits mainly with his wife, Sarah, dealing with the business side of it all. Started a fine arts shop in 1986 when the commissioned work began to fall off. Does well but not brilliantly. Widowed in 1992 when his wife fell from the multistorey car-park.'

'He seemed very cut up about it still,' Sister Joan said.

'He told you they were happy?'

'Yes. He relied on her a lot, I believe.'

'In 1984 the police were called to a domestic disturbance at the Smith house,' Detective Sergeant Mill said without expression.

'Are you sure?'

'According to the records my mate dragged out for me. The police were called out by a neighbour who'd complained of screaming and crashing noises. Anyway they found Mrs Smith – that was Sarah – bruised and cut, but she insisted there'd been an accident and declined to press charges. Odd!'

'What is?'

'They were living at Flat Fifteen, Putney Walk.'

'Where Serge Roskoff lived.'

'Looks like it. They must've moved shortly afterwards and

were living in a flat over his fine arts shop in Chelsea. He didn't mention having lived in Putney Walk?'

'No, he didn't.'

'Anyway the report was kept on file but nothing further transpired.'

'And then Sally was killed.'

'Eight years later?' He raised his eyebrows.

'No connection,' Sister Joan said. 'Of course not. Anyway the two people who saw it happen said that she was alone.'

'Bryan Grimes.' He was reading from his notebook again. 'Born in Lincolnshire in 1956.'

'Sally was born in Lincolnshire too. I'd forgotten that.'

'It's a biggish county. No reason why they should know each other – or did they?'

'When we first arrived at college?' She thought for a moment. 'No, I'm sure that they didn't.'

'Where was I? Yes, here we are. Entered college in 1974, graduated 1977. No definite news about him until 1980 when he started illustrating children's books. He made quite a name for himself it seems. 1984 he was living back in Lincolnshire.'

'And last year he died there.'

'A hit-and-run accident while he was out walking. No known relatives. What was he like?'

'Pleasant, rather quiet.' Sister Joan hesitated, then said, 'During the reunion I heard that Fiona had slept with him. She didn't deny it, but I knew nothing about it at the time.'

'Paul Vance, born in London 1955, entered college in 1974, graduated in '77. No family. Well known as a commercial artist and television personality.'

'I wouldn't know. We don't have television.'

'How civilized it must be in your order,' he said. 'To continue! Finally Serge Roskoff. Came here from Russia as a political refugee during the Cold War. Born 1956, according to his immigration details. Entered college with the rest of you in 1974, graduated in 1977, travelled in Western Europe for several years. Settled in London about six years ago.'

'In Sally and Derek's former flat. Did he lodge with them? I wouldn't've thought there was much room.'

'They'd moved to live over their shop a couple of years before,' he said.

'It seems like a big coincidence.'

'Who knew where Serge Roskoff lived?'

'Paul knew. He'd been in touch several months before. Derek didn't say anything.'

'And Serge Roskoff died last month of a drug overdose. Verdict suicide.'

'I can't believe it!' Sister Joan said with sudden nervous energy. 'Not Serge! He loved life, really gloried in it.'

'People can change. You said that Barbara Ford had.'

'The girl, Patricia, didn't believe it either. And she certainly didn't cut her own throat!'

'There's no logical connection,' he said patiently. 'Serial killers generally use the same methods over and over again. That's why they get caught. Here we have a woman falling out of the top storey of a car-park, a man killed by a hit-and-run driver, a fatal drug overdose with nothing to say it wasn't self-administered, and the very nasty murder of a street waif. It doesn't fit any known scenario.'

'Unless the killer – if there is a killer had to use whatever means were at hand.'

'For what reason?'

'I don't know,' she said helplessly. 'There isn't any reason. We were at art college together where we had our photograph taken and someone said we ought to have a reunion twenty years on. In the intervening time we've all gone our own separate ways.'

'Nobody kept in touch?'

'People ran into people occasionally.'

'And they're all coming down here?'

'For the week's retreat,' Sister Joan said. 'I wish I could feel happier about it.'

'Meaning there's something you haven't told me?' He looked at her sharply.

'When I went to Serge's flat there was a pile of old newspapers there. Patricia said he'd kept them carefully, she didn't know why. I brought them away with me.'

'You should have told me.'

'I'm sorry, but I wanted to take a look at them myself first to see if there was anything in them worth showing, but there doesn't seem to be. Just a list of numbers, dates I think, written down the side margin of one, and here and there an item about one or other of us. I put them up in the library but I can let you have them.'

'You can give them to me when I come and give my talk. That's one reason I drove over here this evening. Will Wednesday afternoon suit you?'

'At three o'clock? Thank you.'

'I'm not as obliging as you think,' he warned. 'I want to take a look at your old comrades.'

'It's still good of you to spare the time. If that's all—? I'm due back in chapel in a few moments.'

She had risen but he lingered at the table, carefully closing his notebook, putting it in his pocket.

'Were the newspapers the only thing you'd neglected to mention?' he asked.

'You do know me well, don't you?' she said resignedly. 'There was this.'

He looked at the photograph she took from her pocket. 'Where did you get this?' he asked sharply.

'Luther had forgotten to give it to me. He offered to bring it up for the postman. Apparently it arrived before the one that reminded me of the reunion. What do you think?'

'At the moment nothing.' He returned it to her, frowning slightly. 'Has anyone else had a marked snapshot?'

'I've no idea. I think someone would have mentioned it if they had.'

'Maybe. Maybe not.' He held open the door as she switched off the light and went through to the front door again.

Walking back to the main building they were both silent. When they reached the main door he spoke abruptly. 'Keep your own counsel, Sister. I'll see you next Wednesday. If anything strikes your memory before then you'll let me know?'

'Yes, of course. Goodnight, Detec— Alan.'

'Goodnight, Sister Joan.'

Glancing back as she went through the main door she saw he was still standing there, his face shadowed.

The final devotion of the day was the recitation of the rosary and the final blessing as each Sister knelt before the prioress to receive the ritual cross traced upon the air and the sprinkling of holy water from the asperges. It marked the start of the grand silence which was broken the next morning when Sister Teresa would whirl her clapper at each door, calling, 'Christ is risen!'

Only in circumstances of the most grave urgency was the grand silence broken. Sister Joan, who twenty years before would have considered herself incapable of remaining silent for seven hours even if some of those hours were spent in sleep, had grown to appreciate the peace and quiet.

Tonight was different. Rising as the cool drops of water sprayed her face, she had an urge to say, 'I would prefer to sleep here tonight, Mother Dorothy. Something out there menaces me. I feel it in my bones.'

She bowed her head, blessed herself, flashed her superior a bright smile, and went out, drawing up the hood of her cloak as she turned in the direction of the door at the end of the chapel passage. This door was, by custom, left unlocked so that anyone seeking spiritual comfort could come into the chapel during the hours of darkness. Once the door that led through to the main living-quarters had been left open too, but Detective Sergeant Mill had insisted it be locked at night for greater security. It was sad to contemplate that even sanctuary required bolts and bars.

She was glad of the emergence of a bright crescent of moon as she went between the high hedges of tangled shrubbery and down the worn steps across the tennis courts. Fitting her key into the lock of the front door of the postulancy she felt for the light switch inside and let out her breath as the narrow hall flooded with light. Until that moment she hadn't realized how tense she was.

Her bag was still in the hall. She bolted the door and took it through into the parlour where a camp bed had been set up and a drawer cleared for her things. The shutters were closed and the bed looked odd stuck against the wall where a narrow shelf held a row of books chosen by Sister Hilaria for her own reading. Sister Joan glanced along the titles without much hope. No Wodehouse or Maureen Lipman here to raise her spirits, only the lives of various saints, all of whom seemed to have met their martyrdoms in the most gruesome manner!

She had better close the shutters upstairs. Going upstairs she switched on the overhead light, which served as illumination for the whole as she went from cell to cell, fastening the shutters into place. That too had been a precaution insisted on by the police.*

Leaning to close the final shutter she paused, looking out. Below, at a little distance Detective Sergeant Mill's car stood, a dark and reassuring bulk in the fragile moonlight. In the back seat she could see the glow of his cigarette as he settled himself for a night's vigil. Touched, she pulled the shutter closed and thanked God for a faithful friend.

* See *Vow of Devotion*.

Seven

'Are we too early?'

Dodie stepped from the long, sleek car and twinkled at Sister Joan with such determination that the latter had a sudden unsettling vision of her twinkling all round the convent, spreading gaiety and irritation like honey left too long in the jar.

'You're just in time for a cup of tea,' she said cordially. 'Derek, there isn't a proper garage any longer, I'm afraid. If you leave your car at the side I can help you carry your bags over to the postulancy.'

'Is that the main house?' Dodie enquired. 'Do we get to see inside it?'

'Yes, of course. You'll be sharing the evening meal with us every day,' Sister Joan said. 'If you'll come this way?'

She would have taken one of the suitcases but Derek had bent to pick up Dodie's neat black one and shouldered his own while Paul carried two, both of maroon leather with his initials in silver on them.

'You didn't bring your own car?' Sister Joan asked him as they started towards the rear of the building.

'Darling, didn't I say?' Paul smiled at her lazily. 'I'm in the last few months of a three-year driving ban. Too much alcohol on an empty stomach if you'll excuse the vulgarism!'

Which surely meant he couldn't have been the one who'd knocked down Bryan Grimes and then driven on without stopping to see how badly Bryan had been injured, unless he'd been driving illegally? Mentally she ordered herself to stop playing amateur detective and behave like a hostess.

'This is the enclosure garden,' she said, nodding towards the low wall. 'You're very welcome to walk or sit there whenever you like. We sell quite a lot of our own fruit and vegetables. That's Sister Martha's domain. She can make anything grow.'

'There are flowers too,' Dodie said.

'For the altar. Oh, while I remember you're welcome in the chapel for any service or simply to sit there and relax. There's a timetable in the postulancy.'

'You're not going to suggest we play tennis, are you?' Paul enquired, looking with disfavour at the weed-rich court with its rusted posts.

'No, but I wish I could,' she said wistfully. 'Nobody's played there for years. If we could get it shipshape again it would be marvellous for exercise.'

'Just imagine all the little novices leaping about with their habits flying up!' Paul said.

'You imagine it,' Sister Joan said coldly.

'It wouldn't raise his temperature one iota,' Dodie said maliciously. 'If they were monks now—'

'Here we are!' Sister Joan raised her voice in determined cheerfulness. 'This is where the novice mistress and the postulants spend most of their time. The postulants spend a year here – at the moment we only have one. She and Sister Hilaria – that's our novice mistress – are camping up in the storeroom next to the library while there are visitors here.'

'We must be an inconvenience to them,' Dodie said with sudden anxiety. 'I do hope it's not a dreadful nuisance our being here.'

'Not in the least. We're all delighted you've come,' Sister Joan said. 'I really didn't expect you to take me up on this retreat business you know.'

'We thought it would be fun to continue the reunion,' Paul said.

'On the right is the meditation room, for anyone who wants some peace and quiet without actually going over to the chapel,' Sister Joan said, feeling like a tour guide. 'My cell is next to it.'

'You're sleeping over here?' Derek looked at her.

'During the retreat, yes. The small kitchen behind is where Sister Teresa and Sister Marie will be making your breakfast.'

'And they are—' Derek looked questioning.

'Sister Teresa is our lay sister. She's responsible for the cooking. She's a super cook so you ought to enjoy the food, and Sister Marie is the novice who helps her. She's just left the postulancy and now she has two years' novitiate to do. It used to be longer but regulations are more relaxed now. Sister Perpetua is our infirmarian and the one to ask if you've got a headache. She looks after Sister Gabrielle and Sister Mary Concepta who are both very elderly and spend most of their time in the infirmary.'

'You remind me of an amusing tale I heard once,' Paul said, lounging against the wall as he drawled out the words. 'A little girl was given a book about penguins and told her teacher, "This book tells me more about penguins than I'll ever need to know".'

'Don't be so bitchy, Paul!' Dodie protested. 'Take no notice of him, Joan! He's been passing nasty comments all the way down! Just like he used to do back in college!'

But in college Paul, as far as she could remember, had been sweet-tempered and gentle. Sister Joan wondered why she should recall him differently from the way in which Dodie described.

'The lecture room is on the left here, with the library and recreation-room next to it,' she said hastily. 'I'm afraid the books are mainly paperbacks. I bought a pile to replace the ones the postulants are allowed to read, and there are jigsaws and Scrabble in the recreation-room, in case it suddenly pours with rain. Would you like to bring your luggage upstairs? Your names are on the doors.'

'I'm surprised you've got men and women accommodated in the same building,' Derek said.

'Mother Dorothy may be moral but she isn't a fool,' Sister Joan said, amused. 'She leaves other people free to lead their lives according to their consciences. Anyway sex isn't always confined to the bedroom, is it?'

'You can assure Mother What'shername that I'm the last person to drag any innocent maiden off into the shrubbery,' Paul said.

'There are two small bathrooms at the end of the passage.' Sister Joan held down the lid on her bubbling temper. 'I'll go down and make you a cup of tea.'

She went downstairs again thankfully, hoping that Paul wasn't going to ruin the entire retreat. She surely would have recalled if he'd been so unpleasant as he was being now when they'd been at college! What had happened to twist his sweet temper into bitterness? There being no immediate answer she put on the kettle and got out the cups and saucers.

The rapping of the knocker sent her to the front door where she was confronted by two heavily burdened figures, Serena in politically incorrect mink, Fiona looking drop-dead gorgeous in a skirt that displayed her long legs and oughtn't to have looked so good on a woman of nearly forty.

'The dearest little nun told us the way to come,' Fiona said. 'She was up a tree.'

'Sister Martha. She's our gardener. Come in. Dodie and Derek and Paul are here.'

'We saw the car at the side,' Serena said, lugging in her suitcases. 'Where shall I put these?'

'Upstairs.' Sister Joan gave the luggage a glance of amused dismay. Serena and Fiona had brought sufficient for a month! She wondered what they expected a retreat to entail.

'This is a lovely place,' Fiona was crying as they ascended. 'Such peace and quiet! Honestly I begin to understand the attractions of a monastic life.'

'Conventual,' Sister Joan said pedantically, her mouth repressing laughter.

'That's only women, right?' Fiona turned her blonde head and gave a large wink. 'No, Sister, I used the right word the first time! There's limits to that there peace and quiet.'

There were sounds of greeting from above, Derek's deeper tones underlining Paul's lighter voice. Sister Joan hurried into the kitchen to add a couple of extra cups and brew the tea. She added biscuits from the tin on the shelf, carried the tray through to the lecture room which would serve as temporary dining-room during the week, and allowed herself to relax for a minute.

The retreat was underway. Nothing she said could stop it or send them all away. At least she'd enjoyed a sound sleep the previous night, waking in the morning to find the sergeant's car gone as unobtrusively as it had arrived. It had been good of him to stay – also faintly troubling since it meant he was more concerned about the situation than he'd been willing to admit.

'Where's the tea then?' Dodie was poking her neatly permed head round the door.

'It's all ready here. Can you look after yourselves for an hour? I have to go out.' She wanted to meet Barbara by herself and seize the chance to ask a few pertinent questions.

'You really can come and go as you please then?' Dodie looked surprised.

'Not exactly. We're not entirely enclosed,' Sister Joan explained. 'The lay sisters usually do the shopping but Sister Teresa doesn't like driving much and Sister Marie is still a novice and confined to the enclosure, so I often go into town to run any errands. The rest can leave when there's grave necessity and with Mother Dorothy's permission. If anyone has a job outside the convent such as teaching or nursing then clearly they're permitted to go to that. Dodie, am I chattering too much about the community?'

'Oh, take no notice of Paul!' Dodie advised. 'If he doesn't want to hear about nuns then he shouldn't have come to a convent!'

'You know I've always rather prided myself on being perceptive about people,' Sister Joan said. 'When we were at college I never guessed that Paul was – oh, I know he didn't date any of us – or did he?'

'Not even Fiona,' Dodie said with a grin that made her look younger, less like a textbook copy of the conventional middle-aged housewife.

'I'd better go. See you later!'

Hurrying back to where the van was parked she realized that not one of them, herself included, had mentioned Serge's death. It was as if his name, his fate, had suddenly become a taboo subject.

Brother Cuthbert came out of the schoolhouse as she drove towards it, flapping his arms.

'Is anything wrong, Brother?' She slowed and stopped.

'Only my own bump of curiosity,' he said. 'Two big cars went by. Have you found visitors for your retreat?'

'Did nobody tell you? I'm so sorry!' She bit her lip in contrition. 'Yes, the old college friends I met in London have come for a week.'

'That's a feather in your cap, Sister!' His honest young face split into a wide beam. 'They must be very fond of you.'

'Fond of me?' She rolled the word round her tongue, feeling it didn't taste right. 'Actually we were none of us particularly close even at college.'

'Then you did a wonderful job of salesmanship, Sister! Congratulations!'

'If I stopped by very often to talk to you, Brother Cuthbert,' she teased, 'I'd soon be confessing the sin of pride! Which reminds me! How would you feel about giving a talk on the monastic life to the visitors? On Tuesday?'

'Sister, I couldn't possibly!'

'I'm sure it wouldn't alter your character for the worse.'

'It isn't that, Sister,' he said earnestly. 'I could talk about the rule and the routine, even relate some very amusing anecdotes but – how can you describe the scent of a flower to somebody who has no sense of smell? I would be inadequate.'

'Whenever I'm tempted to think that I'm getting somewhere in my spiritual life I compare myself with you and tumble off the mountain,' Sister Joan said darkly.

'You will have your wee joke, Sister!' Brother Cuthbert laughed, showing his strong white teeth. 'If you're really wanting to entertain your visitors I'd be happy to play a couple of tunes for them, if that wouldn't be pushing myself forward?'

'That would be marvellous and I ought to have thought of it myself! Sunday afternoon would be nice. The community have a little free time then so they could enjoy it too.'

'Sunday it is, Sister! It's very kind of you to indulge me,' he said. 'Not that your friends won't have heard better performers but as Father Prior is always telling me, when you have a tiny bit of talent you ought to polish it up as a compliment to the Good Lord who gave it to you in the first place.'

Sister Joan nodded and started the van again, thinking privately that if Brother Cuthbert's superior truly believed his talent was tiny then he must be tone deaf!

She drove on into town, parking neatly in the station yard and checking the time on her fob watch.

'Good afternoon, Sister.' A voice broke in upon her thoughts.

'Detective Sergeant – Alan! What an immense surprise to see you,' she said, heavily ironic. 'Have you taken to checking for stolen cars these days?'

'Someone has to keep an eye on you,' he said.

'Look! You're very kind and I did appreciate last night's vigil,' she said, 'but you really can't follow me around everywhere just in case someone tries to bump me off! That marked photograph was probably a spiteful bit of humour. Nothing more.'

'Any ideas who might have sent it?'

'Nothing tangible. That's the problem! There's nothing tangible about any of this, nothing to get your teeth into. But you really don't have to go on mounting guard on me! Believe me, but there's nobody gets up early enough in the morning to catch me!'

'Very modest,' he said, smiling slightly.

'I'll confess it,' she said impatiently. 'Look, I'm on my way to meet Barbara Ford. The others arrived. I can't pretend that I really like them all, but the idea that one of them might actually – well, sorry, but it's not feasible! Derek is clearly still mourning Sally and Dodie and Fiona and Serena wouldn't harm a fly.'

'And Paul Vance?'

'He's come out of the closet with a vengeance,' she said with a grimace. 'But that doesn't mean he's been going round killing people! No, there has to be some other explanation! Someone else.'

'What about the missing link?' He kept pace with her as they went beneath the underpass towards the platforms.

'I beg your pardon?'

'The person who took the photograph,' he said. 'Think about it, Sister.'

'I can't remember who took it,' Sister Joan said. 'I'd forgotten all about even having had it taken until it arrived! Shall I ask one of the others?'

'Wait a while. See if anybody mentions it. Are you still going to be sleeping over in the postulancy?'

'There's a lock on my door which I intend to use,' she assured him. 'You don't have to miss any more sleep.'

'You'll take care?'

'I always do.' She lifted her hand in a half salute and walked on, aware that he was frowning after her.

The London train was just drawing in. She watched the passengers alight, gripped suddenly by the irrational fear that Barbara wouldn't be there. Then she saw her, dark hair gleaming, emerald-green trouser suit the last word in elegance as she stepped on to the platform and looked round.

'There you are! I was wondering if this place ran to a taxi in case you hadn't come. Are the others here yet? I had the most damnable journey. Two old dears who sucked peppermints very noisily and kept yelling across me.'

Her smile was wide, her voice light and cheerful. No trace here of mousy Barbara who had left college to nurse a seriously ill father who hadn't been ill at all.

'I'm afraid you'll have to put up with the old van,' Sister Joan said aloud. 'We used to have an even older car but Brother Cuthbert adores delving into engines so we did a swap with him. We have supper at seven, so you've plenty of time to change and settle in.'

There was no sign of Detective Sergeant Alan Mill as they went beneath the underpass towards the car-park, but she would have laid odds on his having had a splendid view of the newcomer already.

'It looks very nice,' Barbara said politely as they reached the vehicle.

'It looked nicer before,' Sister Joan said. 'I painted murals all over it but Mother Dorothy had a fit and made me repaint it all grey. However it gets us from place to place. Make yourself comfortable.'

'Brother Cuthbert's your tame hermit, isn't he?'

'Brother Cuthbert is a treasure.' Sister Joan slid behind the wheel. 'I met him when I went up to Scotland on a retreat and it was a real pleasure when he came down to Cornwall to do his sabbatical.'*

'And the others are here.' Barbara adjusted her seatbelt and shot Sister Joan a questioning look.

'They came early.'

'Saying nothing about anything, I suppose?'

'Anything?'

'Serge being dead,' Barbara said. 'When you telephoned and told us it was a nasty shock, cast a gloom over the rest of the day. I'll bet nobody's mentioned him though since they all arrived.'

* See *Vow of Sanctity*

'Not a word.'

'I can't believe that Serge killed himself,' Barbara said vehemently. 'He was always so full of life. Moody, yes, but I used to think he put that on because Russians are supposed to be moody and emotional sometimes. He was so kind.'

'He had a girlfriend,' Sister Joan said carefully. 'Did you know?'

'I assumed he had heaps of them,' Barbara said.

'A girl called Patricia Mayne. I met her briefly when I went to his flat. She was more like a protégé, I think, very young and very lonely. Serge had been kind to her and she repaid him in the only coin she had.'

'Nice to know he had someone,' Barbara commented. 'I suppose she's terribly upset?'

'She's dead,' Sister Joan said flatly.

'Dead? But you said—?'

'That I met her. Yes. She was killed round about midnight on the same evening. Someone found her in Putney Walk with her throat cut.'

She had given the unvarnished truth, hoping for a reaction. For an instant there was silence. Then Barbara said in a choked voice, 'Please can we stop for a moment? Just stop?'

'Yes, of course.'

Sister Joan steered the van on to a grass verge and Barbara unsnapped her seatbelt, wrenched open the van door and was promptly violently sick, her head leaning over the grass, her face chalk white.

'Come and sit on the step!' Sister Joan hastily alighted from the driving seat, snatching a box of tissues as she did so, and came round to the passenger side. 'Here! I've a small bottle of mineral water in the back. I'll get it. I'm sorry. I didn't realize it'd affect you so badly.'

'I'm all right.' Barbara wiped her mouth, drank from the bottle of water, and sat up straighter, her face gradually regaining a tinge of colour. 'I can't bear hearing about violence, that's all. I never could. I'm so sorry.'

Under the exquisite make-up and smart suit the old Barbara, shy, quiet and apologetic showed momentarily, then was gone as she lifted her head, stepped back up into the van again, and reached for her seatbelt. Only the faint tremor of the pink-tipped fingers betrayed her.

'Are you sure you're all right?'

Starting the van again Sister Joan sent her a worried look.

'Fine. Sorry to be so squeamish.' Barbara gave a pale smile. 'Poor girl! Let's not talk about it any more, or mention it to the others! This is going to be a happy week!'

'Of course it is.' Sister Joan turned off onto the moorland road, storing away for future reference the fact that Barbara hadn't asked if anyone had yet been arrested for the girl's murder.

'What a glorious view!' she exclaimed a moment later. 'You're lucky to live here.'

'Yes, it's beautiful.' Sister Joan kept her tone casual and cheerful. Now wasn't the moment to ask why Barbara had lied about her father.

'Do you do a lot of painting?' the other was asking.

'Not very often,' Sister Joan confessed. 'One has to have permission and anyway there's always so much else to do. That small building over there is the old school. It belongs to the community and I used to teach the local kids there when I first came, but the council closed it down and laid on a bus to take them to the school in town, so now Brother Cuthbert is spending a year there.'

There was, however, no sign of Brother Cuthbert. Probably he'd been too shy to stay visible in the face of another visitor.

'Here we are!' Sister Joan drove through the gates and round to the yard where the van lived under a stretched awning in lieu of garage.

'Is this the last one?' Sister Perpetua came out of the kitchen, wiping her hands on her apron. 'Welcome to our community.'

'Barbara Ford, Sister Perpetua, our infirmarian,' Sister Joan made the introduction.

'Miss Ford.' Sister Perpetua shook hands briskly. 'You look a little pale!'

'Barbara was travel sick.'

'Then I've just the thing! Come into the kitchen and we'll have you feeling better in a trice,' Sister Perpetua said, cheering up visibly at the prospect of a patient. 'You run along, Sister, and round up the others! Miss Ford can sit quietly and get her breath back.'

Barbara had been taken in tow, Sister Perpetua being completely unfazed by the exquisite make-up and elegant suit. Sister Joan lingered to give Lilith a pat on the nose and the whispered promise of a canter soon, then went with somewhat mixed feelings over to the postulancy, hailed on her way by Derek who was halfway up a ladder in the garden picking the last few apples from the top of the tree, while Sister Martha stood meekly below with her basket.

'As you can see,' he called, leaning out at a dangerous angle, 'I'm making myself useful!'

'He did offer,' Sister Martha put in.

'I didn't think you'd dragged him over the wall against his will,' Sister Joan quipped and walked on.

Perhaps the retreat wasn't going to be so bad after all. She would take each day as it came.

A lilac dusk was already edging the postulancy. Lights were on everywhere. She hoped that the modest fees the visitors were paying would leave something over when the week's electricity bill had been paid. Silly to worry about that when in the background something hovered, something deadly. Four people dead, the last definitely murdered, Barbara's lie about her father, Paul's unexpected malice. The photograph with its brutal black crosses and the circle round her own youthful face.

She shook her head slightly and went in. Serena, wearing an expensive dinner dress and contriving to make it look like a reject from a thrift shop, was in the lecture room, collecting up cups and saucers.

'I thought I'd lend a hand,' she said amiably as Sister Joan looked in. 'Paul went off for a walk by himself and Fiona wanted to have a look at the chapel.'

'Where's Dodie?'

'Upstairs, getting herself ready for dinner – or is it supper? I won't be eating very much so do please explain that it's no reflection on the food, merely that I'm slimming, will you?'

'Yes of course I will,' Sister Joan said gravely, and went on up the stairs.

The door of Dodie's room was barely ajar. She tapped and pushed it open as Dodie whirled round, clutching a bathrobe about her.

'Am I late? I decided to take a quick bath,' she said anxiously.

'No. There's plenty of time. I'll see you later.'

Going out again, the smile stiffening on her face, she wondered what on earth had caused the blue and yellow bruises on Dodie's shoulders.

Eight

Supper was more elaborate than usual, something for which the community could thank the presence of the visitors. There was watercress soup, a poached salmon with new potatoes and buttered asparagus, and a summer pudding with cream. There was also a glass of wine by each plate. By the visitors' plates, Sister Joan corrected, sipping her drink and finding raspberry juice. An extra table had been put up in the refectory for the six visitors with a chair for Sister Joan at the head of it.

From her own chair at the adjoining table Mother Dorothy said, 'This is the first opportunity I have had of welcoming you all here. Sister Joan will have told you something of our lives here. At supper we have a reading from a suitable book so that we have something to concentrate our minds while we eat. Sister Katherine is to read from the life of Elizabeth of Hungary whose story is very moving. Let us begin with grace.'

Rising, bowing her head, Sister Joan wondered if any of the lay visitors present were in the habit of saying grace! From the slightly embarrassed looks she glimpsed, none of them! And why Saint Elizabeth of Hungary? The story of a young wife giving bread to the poor against the orders of her husband and having the bread turned into roses when she was forced to open her apron was hardly intellectually stimulating.

'Are we allowed to talk?' Fiona demanded in a stage whisper as Sister Katherine paused for breath.

Sister Joan shook her head, feeling like a school monitor as Fiona made a rueful face.

She would have liked to enjoy her meal but too many questions buzzed in her mind. Dodie's bruises didn't look recent but they looked horrific. Had she been in an accident? If so surely she'd have mentioned it! Barbara's sickness – why had she had such an extreme reaction to the news of the death of someone she'd never heard of before? Why had Paul become so malicious, so serpent-tongued? Why, why, why?

'Mass is at seven in the morning if anyone wishes to attend.'

Mother Dorothy was speaking again and Sister Joan hadn't even noticed Sister Katherine sit down to begin her own meal.

'Is it permitted to congratulate the cook?' Derek enquired. 'I think I speak for all of us when I say the meal was delicious.'

'Sister Teresa and Sister Marie will be happy to treasure the compliment,' Mother Dorothy said graciously. 'The community now goes to recreation. Then we go into chapel for the final blessing at ten. We look forward to seeing you all again tomorrow. Sister Joan, you will remember that you are still bound by the grand silence after the blessing, except in cases of grave emergency.'

Sister Joan murmured an assent, wondering indignantly if the prioress expected her to sit up all night gossiping with her old friends.

'So what entertainment is laid on now?' Paul enquired, as she shepherded them down into the main hall.

'There are books and board games over in the postulancy,' Sister Joan said, feeling like a fool as she met Paul's raised eyebrows. 'If anyone wishes to take a walk or go into town then that's fine. The front gate isn't locked and I'll sit up until the last one comes in.'

'St Joan the Martyr,' Paul said. 'We'll be back by eleven. Anyone coming for a drink?'

He looked at the others who shook their heads.

'There's no sense in coming on a retreat and dashing off to sink pints in the local tavern,' Derek said.

'Actually I was thinking of a cocktail,' Paul said. 'Nobody? Right, I'll take myself off then. See you all later.'

'Why does he have to be so sneering?' Fiona said, watching the slim figure recede into the darkness.

'Let's walk over to the postulancy.' Dodie sounded bright. 'I don't suppose that there's a television set or a radio?'

'Sorry.'

'Actually I don't much mind. Colin watches it all the time but I can take it or leave it,' Dodie said.

'Mother Dorothy does take a newspaper,' Sister Joan said.

Surely somebody had read about Patricia Mayne's murder in a newspaper or heard about it from the radio or television? She supposed that there were many violent acts reported these days and none of them had any reason to connect the killing of an unknown girl with the death of Serge Roskoff.

'Scrabble!' Fiona said brightly as they went into the postulancy.

'Fiona, your spelling is as good as your painting,' Dodie said.

'I can spell bitch,' Fiona said so tartly that Sister Joan jumped, 'and I haven't descended to designing Christmas cards yet.'

'Those who can paint, paint. Those who can't paint, teach art,' Dodie said.

'Oh, do stop bickering!' Serena said, yawning. 'Honestly this is supposed to be a nice peaceful few days! So why are we on edge?'

'Because Serge died?' Sister Joan introduced the name, glancing from face to face. Barbara had sat down, one hand shielding her face; Dodie drew in her head sharply as if she was offended; Serena and Fiona looked down at their hands. For a moment nobody spoke. Then Fiona said, 'We haven't talked about it. There didn't seem anything to say.'

'He didn't do drugs,' Sister Joan said.

'How do you know?' Dodie asked. 'You hadn't seen him for years. None of us had.'

'Paul was in touch, wasn't he?'

'Only vaguely,' Serena said. 'Wasn't he thinking of featuring Serge's work in an arts programme? Nothing came of it though.'

'Serge died last month,' Sister Joan said. 'It's odd that none of you heard about it. I mean, he did have some success in the early years, didn't he? Don't any of you read the newspapers or watch television?'

There was silence still. Barbara was frowning, her hand now plucking the edge of her green sweater.

'We did know,' she said. 'At least I knew and Paul knew. I can't speak for the rest.'

'Then why didn't you say anything?' Sister Joan looked at her in astonished hurt. 'Why on earth did you let me go traipsing off to his flat if you already knew he was dead?'

'We hoped you might find out something,' Barbara said.

'Find out what?'

'Something. Anything. There was a bit in the newspaper ages ago mentioning that a Sister Joan had helped the police to catch a murderer. A gypsy child?'*

'I didn't know my name had appeared anywhere,' Sister Joan said with distaste. 'It certainly wasn't with my permission! But when we met on the train you looked surprised to see that I was a nun!'

'Sorry,' said Barbara.

'Sorry!' Sister Joan echoed. 'Barbara, if you knew I'd entered a convent why not simply say so. Why pretend?'

'Habit,' Barbara said abruptly.

'You were the one who set the camera.' The memory had come out of nowhere. 'That's why your face was blurred in the photograph. You set it up and rushed to join the rest of us before the timer clicked. You set the photograph up.'

'I don't see what that has to do with anything,' Serena said, puzzled.

'Never mind!' Sister Joan looked at them wearily. 'It doesn't matter. You wanted this reunion so you sent round the photograph. It was you, wasn't it?'

'No.' Barbara shook her head. 'No, I didn't send it round.'

'I don't believe any of us did,' Fiona said blankly.

'Somebody did!' Derek who had been staring through the window turned abruptly, his dark face angry. 'Somebody got us all together! Why? So we could enjoy a reunion?'

'What other reason could there be?' Fiona asked.

'I have to go to chapel!' Sister Joan cast a glance at her fob watch. 'After that it's the grand silence. It doesn't apply to you, of course, but it means I can't speak save in the gravest emergency until five-thirty tomorrow morning.'

'I think I need some air,' Fiona said, 'but I'm nervous about walking in the dark alone.'

'There are torches in the kitchen,' Sister Joan began. 'You can use one.'

'I'll come with you,' Derek offered.

'So will I!' Dodie had spoken too quickly.

* See *Vow of Chastity*

'I'll see you all later then.'

It was with a definite feeling of relief that she turned and hurried out. They had known about Serge – or at least Barbara and Paul had known, yet they'd still allowed her to go to his flat. They'd hoped she find out something, she supposed. But what? That he hadn't committed suicide? Sister Joan Super Sleuth, she thought without mirth. Reunion my foot! She was being used but by whom exactly and for what eventual purpose she simply didn't know.

Once they had all been friends – not perhaps close friends but working together, attending lectures together. To her mind such a bond demanded a certain faithfulness. Fidelity was a cornerstone of friendship. It struck her that they hadn't shown much either to her or to each other. Perhaps she had lived too long in the community where despite small clashes of personality any one of the sisters would have died for any one of the others! In the world everything was different.

Father Malone had told her once that scrupulosity was a sin of the conscience, a deliberate dwelling on small faults that in itself could be an occasion for pride.

I can't judge others by my own standards, she thought, turning in at the chapel door, trying to fit her mind to the rhythm of the final blessing of the day, but even as the beads of her rosary slid through her fingers the questions continued to come.

Why was Dodie so dreadfully bruised? Why had she seemed so cross when Derek had offered to accompany Fiona on her stroll? Fiona was a beautiful woman, Derek a handsome widower. If the two of them got together it would make one happy ending. Yet Dodie had behaved like a jealous woman!

And Barbara! Mousy Barbara Ford whose father hadn't recovered from any illness and who certainly hadn't remarried and gone to New Zealand. Barbara had known that she was a nun, had known that Serge was dead. She had tried to draw her into something without being honest about it. And Barbara had been most deeply and terribly shocked when she'd learned of Patricia Mayne's death. Nobody could fake vomiting.

'*In nomine patris et filii*—'

Mother Dorothy's voice drew a line through the remaining questions. Sister Joan rose, moved up the aisle with the others and knelt to receive the blessing, carefully making her face a sweet blank. There was absolutely no point in worrying her superior with this mishmash of half-formed suspicions when Mother Dorothy was so anxious for the retreat to be a success.

The grand silence came almost always as a welcome friend, making it impossible to discuss, request or argue. It was a time when troubles could be seen in perspective, when the sounds of living were muted. Tonight she wanted to rush back to the postulancy and submit everybody to the third degree!

She turned aside towards the open ground that stretched to the low wall. The moon had emerged and there was no need of other light. Since it was unlikely that Paul would return until he'd drunk his fill in the pub and presumably the others were still out for a stroll there was no rush for her to go indoors.

Alice came bounding up, licking her hand. She stroked the dog absently, her glance sharpening as pinpoints of light hovered beyond the wall. Had all the visitors gone out with torches then? Stepping closer to the boundary wall she watched the line of lights and heard the voices calling.

'Finn! Finn, where are you? Finn!'

Men's voices echoing across the moor. She strained to hear more, gripped by a sudden foreboding.

'Sister Joan, is that you?'

Padraic Lee had reached her, shining his torch and making her blink.

She nodded, her finger to her lips.

'I know you're not supposed to talk at this hour,' he said. 'It's young Finn Boswell. He went off to play this afternoon and he's not back yet. His mam's getting fretted about him. He's her own one and she fusses. D'ye know the boy?'

She shook her head.

'He's a nice little lad,' Padraic said, trying not to sound worried. 'Only seven years old. Dark, like all the Boswells. Not a naughty boy at all, but then kids will take it into their heads to wander, won't they? You don't think he might have gone into your chapel and fallen asleep or something?'

She shook her head again.

'Oh well, I reckon he'll turn up sooner or later,' Padraic said. 'Sorry to bother you, Sister. Tell Sister Teresa that I've some nice herrings on order for next week, will you? Half price to her, of course.'

Since they'd probably fallen off the back of a lorry in the first place, she reflected, half price was fair according to Padraic's curious moral code.

The lights were arching away again, paling under the moon, the voices diminishing as Padraic loped back. The Romanies were fiercely fond of their children. They would search until Finn was found.

A child missing. A child missing. The words repeated themselves in her head, over and over. A child missing. She had read that phrase recently but where? Children often went missing these days. It was one of the most unpleasant facts of life.

Ten years before a child had gone missing. She'd seen the item in one of the newspapers she'd brought home from Serge's flat. Sheer coincidence. Nothing to do with anything! Nothing at all! Finn Boswell would turn up safe and well, like that other little boy – or had that other child been found? She couldn't recall having noticed anything about it. Then she'd been looking for something connected with the college students with whom Serge had mingled.

Turning, she went back towards the chapel, going in through the unlocked door at the side. By now the connecting door to the living-quarters would be locked and the door to the big storeroom that had been adapted for Sister Hilaria and Sister Bernadette would be locked too. She entered the chapel where the sanctuary lamp glowed scarlet, casting a mellow glow over the carpet on the altar steps. She genuflected, walked softly to the Lady Altar and mounted the spiral stairs at the side of it.

On the landing above a light switch turned on a low wattage bulb. She turned it on, went softly into the remaining storeroom with its piled boxes, its narrow aisle under the skylight. The newspapers were still here. She picked them up, found a carrier bag and slid them inside. As she turned off the landing light and went down the stairs again she reflected that the grand silence didn't forbid reading.

Serena and Dodie were playing Scrabble in the recreation-room when she looked in, the latter raising a welcoming hand before continuing to shuffle the letters. There was no sign of the others. Obviously Dodie had returned early from the stroll or hadn't bothered to go at all.

She went into her own room across the hall, sliding the bolt on the inside of the door and spreading out the newspapers on the table.

There had been several missing children during the last ten years – too many – and, in most cases, their stories weren't even followed up but elbowed aside by fresh, more sensational stories. Here was the item she'd noticed!

LONDON SCHOOLBOY MISSING

Johnny Clare, the nine-year-old schoolboy from Chelsea, has now been missing for three days and police are becoming increasingly concerned for his safety. Johnny, a pupil at Cheyne High School, apparently played truant last Thursday afternoon. He had previously missed the occasional lesson but was not, according to his form master, an habitual truant. When he left the school premises after lunch he told a prefect who enquired that he had an errand to run. When he didn't return to his home in Cheyne Walk, his mother assumed he had lingered to play with friends but by eight o'clock when there was still no sign of him his parents began telephoning round and at nine o'clock informed the police. Preliminary enquiries established he had not returned to school that afternoon, had no errand to run, and had not been seen subsequently by any of his friends.

Johnny was wearing jeans, trainers with a red logo on the heels, and a blue jersey over a white T-shirt. He is four feet nine inches in height, of slim build with a fresh complexion and brown hair and eyes. He is an adopted child but has known about that since he was a toddler and is happy and well adjusted.

His father, Henry Clare, an engineer, has offered a substantial reward for any information leading to the return of his son.

'If anyone knows anything at all,' Mr Clare told our reporter, 'we wish to hear it. Johnny is a friendly child but he's sensible and unlikely to go off with a stranger. His mother and I think the world of him and would do anything for news.'

The next reference was in a paper of the following week and was briefer.

MISSING SCHOOLBOY

Hope is fading for the safe return of Johnny Clare, the nine-year-old Chelsea schoolboy who went missing from his school ten days ago. No useful information has been received since he left the school premises at lunchtime. His adoptive parents, Mr and Mrs Henry Clare, have offered a substantial reward.

There was a small head and shoulders photograph of Johnny. Sister Joan looked at it closely. He had been a pleasant-featured child with a lock of hair cowlicking his brow and a frank, open expression on his childish face.

The next three newspapers had nothing about the missing child. Her heart sank as she riffled through them. Obviously there had been other more exciting events to place before the public. Johnny Clare had become one of the army of shadowy missing people whose relatives occasionally surfaced on television programmes begging for news when all the signs were that their loved ones were beyond the giving or getting of any information.

Perhaps she was on the wrong track. Serge had kept the newspapers for no other reason than that there were glancing references in them to his old college friends.

BODY OF MISSING SCHOOLBOY FOUND

Her eyes lit on the headline and she felt a dart of sick excitement. Johnny had been found then. Suddenly she didn't want to know what had happened to him. Reading about the case made her a voyeur, poking her fingers into other people's tragedies. Yet it was impossible not to read the item.

The remains of a child found buried in a field on the outskirts of Maidstone in Kent have been identified as Johnny Clare, the nine-year-old schoolboy from Chelsea, who disappeared six years ago. Preliminary reports indicate that the boy was sexually

assaulted and then had his throat cut. Forensic scientists are now
making more detailed examinations. The news was given to his
adoptive parents by Christchurch police, the Clares having
emigrated to New Zealand three months ago.

It was all there if only she could see it as a whole, and not in
little snippets, odd names and words that matched if only she
had the key.

She flicked tremblingly through the other newspapers but
there was nothing more about Johnny Clare, no account of
anyone 'helping the police with their enquiries', no interview
with the bereaved parents. There was a brief item reporting the
tragic death of Sarah Smith, 'wife of the portrait painter Derek
Smith' and another longer item about Bryan Grimes, 'the
well-known illustrator of children's books', and that seemed to
be all.

One thing was certain. The newspapers would have to be
given to Detective Sergeant Mill before he came to give his
lecture on Wednesday afternoon. She would ask Mother
Dorothy if she could take Lilith for a gallop after mass in the
morning. She was more likely to get permission for that than
for driving the van on the Sabbath.

There were voices in the hall, the sound of the front door
closing. She slipped the newspapers back into the carrier bag,
thrust it under her camp bed and opened the door.

'There you are, Sister dear!' Paul stood in the narrow
hallway, his eyes over-bright, his mouth twisting slightly.

She nodded, a finger to her lips, and raised her brows
questioningly.

'Ah! The grand silence has begun!' he said mockingly. 'Will
you save your scolding for me until the morning? I've had a
couple too many I fear. I never could resist ye olde worlde
hostelry with a plethora of fake beams! I saw lights on the
moor. Most romantic! I don't know if anyone else is out or not. I
saw nobody and kept my own counsel!'

He put a long finger to his nose and went on up the stairs,
leaving her to stare after him. Whatever he had taken hadn't
been alcohol, she thought. There was no smell on his breath,
nothing to suggest the faint thickening of the voice that alcohol

caused, not the smallest unsteadiness in his gait. Cocaine? Pep pills? She had no idea of the immediate effect of such drugs.

'Was that Paul?' Serena came out of the recreation-room, yawning. 'I'm going up to bed now. The car drive made me so tired. 'Night.'

She waggled her fingers and went slowly up the stairs.

Sister Joan went into the recreation-room where Dodie was putting away the Scrabble set neatly. Dodie had always been neat. Had Sister Joan been asked to predict the future course of Dodie's life she would have guessed marriage to a professional man, two children, her talent bringing in a little extra money to be used for family treats. The bruises told another story. Did the estimable Colin come home from work and batter Dodie sometimes? Wife-beating wasn't confined to the slums. Dodie lived in Maidstone. It was in a field outside Maidstone that poor little Johnny Clare had been found. Johnny Clare, adopted son of Henry Clare, engineer. Dodie's husband was an engineer. There were apparent links that might not be links at all.

Dodie looked up, opened her mouth to say something, then closed it again. Sister Joan gave her an encouraging nod, designed to convey that the visitors weren't bound by any rule of silence, but Dodie shook her head, turning suddenly to the box of Scrabble, her small fingers darting into the bag of letters.

The letters were laid on the table, her fingers adjusting them, and then she was gone, almost running from the room.

LOCK YOUR DOOR. Only that. Sister Joan stared down at them, then swept them back into the bag. She would certainly lock her door. She wondered why Dodie had suddenly been impelled to warn her.

'Anyone at home?' Fiona poked her blonde head round the door. 'Oh, there you are! I know you're not allowed to talk but do they let you listen?'

Sister Joan nodded.

'Barbara came with us in the end,' Fiona said, seating herself and looking with disfavour at a rip in her tights. 'Dodie decided to stay in and play Scrabble. We walked for ages. Derek took one of the torches but the moonlight was quite bright in places. We're late because we ran into a crowd of gypsies, all looking for a child who hadn't gone home. Derek and Barbara offered to go with them to search and I said I'd come back and tell you not to wait up because Barbara says she'll lock the front door when they get in and you have to get up at some unearthly hour! Is there a cup of tea going?'

Sister Joan nodded and went out, crossing to the small kitchen, busying herself. At her heels Fiona was hovering, her voice light and quick, her breathing rapid.

'You know I do think that the others have changed terribly! I hardly recognized Barbara and Paul is grown so spiteful! I do hope they're not going to spoil things for the rest of us during this retreat!'

Sister Joan hoped nobody was going to spoil anything but had the gravest doubts. One thing at least was clear to her. Some of those who were here intended to make use of her in order to discover the truth behind Serge Roskoff's death. Barbara, at least, had finally admitted it. She wondered if Fiona was party to anything. Fiona was so pretty and scatterbrained that people mistakenly regarded her as stupid.

'Well, I'll not worry you again,' Fiona chattered, taking the tea. 'Oh, I think I can hear Barbara and Derek coming back. I wonder if they've found that little boy.'

Derek had opened the front door and ushered Barbara within. Both looked tired and slightly windswept.

'Not a sign of the kid,' Barbara said. 'The others – the gypsies said they'd go on looking all night. I told them they ought to report it to the police but they don't seem too keen on that idea.'

'I believe gypsies usually steer clear of the law,' Derek said, looking amused.

'Even so!' Fiona said. 'When it's a child—'

'Who will probably turn up safe and sound having spent the night poaching,' Derek soothed. 'Is there any more tea where that came from? I'm parched.'

'Speaking of thirst is Paul back?' Barbara enquired. 'We saw his car.'

'My car.' Derek looked slightly annoyed.

'Yes, your car.' Barbara nodded and went into the kitchen.

Sister Joan pointed to the ceiling and nodded to indicate that everybody was in, and went to the front door to bolt it.

As she turned to watch the three of them go across into the

recreation-room, when she thought of the three who had already gone upstairs, she couldn't help wondering if she had just bolted danger out or in.

Nine

It wasn't until she'd tethered Lilith in the yard at the side of the police station that she realized that on Sunday morning Detective Sergeant Mill was unlikely to be at his desk. Mother Dorothy had given permission for the ride without question, adding, 'As long as our guests are not neglected I see no reason why you shouldn't take a short break from time to time, and Lilith is in need of a good gallop.'

Sister Teresa and Sister Marie had gone over to the postulancy to make a light breakfast for the guests, only one of whom had surfaced. As she went through the front door Paul, in a dressing-gown of such vivid hues it would have made Liberace cringe, called from the head of the stairs, 'Good morning! Any chance of getting some Sunday newspapers?'

'I'll see what I can do. How are you this morning?'

'Fine. Shouldn't I be?'

'Good,' Sister Joan said coldly, and went out into the early morning air.

Paul had followed her, his dressing-gown clashing with the pale gold of the morning.

'You sound cross, Sister dear,' he said.

'I was hoping nobody would bring dope here,' she said frankly.

'I didn't.' He spread his hands palm up. 'I keep a teeny-weeny supply in the car.'

'In Derek's car. Does he know?'

'Oh, he doesn't mind.' He sounded so casual that her irritation increased.

Sharply she said, 'Look! Don't you have a driving ban? That was why you came down with Derek, right? You drove off down to the village happily enough last night.'

'Why didn't you stop me?'

'Because I didn't think of it at the time. Are you going to drive again?'

'Probably not.' He sent her a lazy smile. 'If you really insist I'll stay off the dope too.'

'That,' said Sister Joan with asperity, 'would be appreciated!'

The moor had been deserted. No sign of searchers combing the bracken. No sign of Brother Cuthbert either who, in any case, generally spent Sundays in meditation and prayer once he had attended mass in the parish church. Perhaps Finn Boswell had been found safe and well. Her spirits lifted at the thought, and she allowed Lilith to have her head, tearing over the short, autumn-browned grass while Sister Joan, the skirt of her habit flying up, blessed Mother Dorothy for having had the good sense to allow her to wear jeans under her habit when she went riding.

The town had a Sunday feeling. From first one steeple, then another, bells pealed. She stopped at a newsagent's and bought a selection of Sunday newspapers, loaded them into the saddle-bag, tethered Lilith to the post and went into the station, the carrier bag containing the old newspapers in her hand.

'Good morning, Sister Joan.' Constable Petrie raised his head from the tabloid spread out before him on the reception desk. 'Nothing wrong up at the convent I hope?'

'Nothing at all, Constable. I brought these in for Detective Sergeant Mill to see. Can you see that he gets them?'

'You can give them to him yourself, Sister,' the young constable said. 'He's in his office.'

'Oh! Thank you.' She moved to the half-glass door and tapped on it.

'Sister Joan!' He looked up from the notes he was making with an expression of pleased surprise. 'This is an unexpected pleasure! Sit down!'

'I brought the newspapers in that I took from Serge's flat. I didn't know you worked on Sundays.'

She put the carrier bag on the table and sat down.

'One Sunday in three. It's generally a very quiet day. After Saturday night the local criminals take a holiday! Have you found anything in these?'

'One or two odd coincidences. The little boy who was abducted and found dead years later – Johnny Clare?'

'I don't think I recall the case. Bring me up to date and tell me what it has to do with your present concerns – that's if you have time?'

'A limited amount.' She folded her hands in her lap and hesitated.

Detective Sergeant Mill had complimented her once that she gave evidence more clearly and concisely than anyone he knew outside the Force. At this moment she felt inadequate, too many imponderables muddling her thinking.

'Take your time,' he encouraged.

'Ten years ago a nine-year-old schoolboy from Chelsea was abducted and not found until six years later when his remains were discovered in a field near Maidstone in Kent. His throat had been cut. As far as I know nobody was ever arrested for the crime.'

'Now I remember it.' He nodded, frowning. 'The child's body had been rather better preserved than is usual. Some minerals in the soil or something. Didn't they find out he'd been assaulted?'

'Yes, poor child!' Instinctively she raised her hand to bless herself, caught the detective sergeant's agnostic eye, and continued hastily, 'He was an adopted child. His father, adoptive father I mean, was Henry Clare, an engineer. By the time the body was found the Clares had given up hope and returned to New Zealand.'

'Where your friend, Barbara Ford, went.'

'After her father didn't remarry,' Sister Joan said.

'Have you asked her about that yet?'

'There hasn't been the right moment. She has admitted that she and Paul both knew that Serge was dead before I went to his flat.'

'Then why let you go?'

'Apparently they'd seen my name in connection with something I'd helped out with and decided that I might be useful in some way. The reunion provided them with the opportunity to involve me. I was naturally curious about Serge's suicide and I naturally began asking questions. In other words they tried to use me!'

'Would you have helped if they'd asked you outright?' he enquired.

'I'm not sure.' She rose abruptly and went over to the window to stare through the frosted panes at the vague outlines of the yard. 'I'm a nun, not a detective! My first duty is to the community.'

'I thought it was to God,' he observed mildly.

'Yes, of course. That goes without saying!' She swung round impatiently. Her fists clenched. 'I am not a free agent, Alan! I must be faithful to the vows that I made before anything else. Old comradeship is no more than an exercise in nostalgia. I can't indulge in it.'

'But you want to find out the truth?'

'Yes. Yes I do.' She came back to the chair and sat down abruptly. 'Someone wanted to get us all together for this reunion. Someone sent round the photographs. Oh, it was Barbara who took the photograph. The camera had one of those timing devices and she set it and barely got into her place before the flash went off. Her face is a bit blurred. She says she didn't send the photograph round. They all say that. And Serge didn't because he'd had one sent to him.'

'The girl Patricia Mayne told you that?'

'Yes. She mentioned the newspapers too.' Sister Joan was struck by a thought. 'Do you think she was there to pique my curiosity further with her hints about Serge not having committed suicide?'

'I doubt if they're all in league to draw you into their amateur investigations,' he said.

'You're right. I'm starting to feel paranoid,' she admitted ruefully. 'It's just that some of them seem so – altered. I know people do mature, change a little, but Barbara has a hard, brilliant edge to her that I'd never have thought she'd acquire in a thousand years, and Paul – Paul used to be so nice, Alan! I didn't know he was gay then. Twenty years ago people weren't as open about such things as they are today. He was gentle and rather sweet-natured, and now he's bitchy and mocking, and so is Dodie.'

'But she's not gay?'

'Married. Her husband Colin Mason is an engineer and they live in Maidstone.'

'Interesting.' He had made the connection and was jotting something down on a piece of paper.

'Her shoulders are covered with bruises,' Sister Joan said tensely. 'I walked in on her when she was changing for supper and though she quickly pulled up her robe I saw them clearly. I haven't asked her about them. Last night I thought she wanted to say something to me privately but the grand silence had begun. She took some letters from the Scrabble game and made a sentence. Lock your door. Just those three words.'

'I trust that you did,' he said mildly.

'I didn't want anyone finding the newspapers,' she said.

'And you've looked through them again?' He reached for the carrier bag, drew out the papers and glanced up at her.

'Only the items about Johnny Clare.'

'Why?'

'Because of the little boy going missing from the gypsy camp.'

'There's a child missing from there?'

'Yes. Surely they've reported it!' Sister Joan experienced a moment's bewilderment before she exclaimed, her brow clearing, 'Obviously he's home safely. The men from the camp were out on the moor looking for him last night.'

'And you connected one child with another? That's rather strange logic.'

'It wasn't logic at all,' she protested. 'It was simply instinct. I didn't connect them in any real sense. It was simply that when Padraic told me there was a child missing I vaguely recalled seeing something about a missing child in one of the old newspapers and I looked it up. And there were links between Johnny Clare and the class I was in in 1974!'

'Very tenuous ones,' he objected.

'Barbara Ford went to New Zealand and Johnny's adoptive parents came from there and went back there when they'd given up hope of finding Johnny. Henry Clare was an engineer and Dodie married an engineer, and she lives in Maidstone where Johnny's remains were found.'

'New Zealand is a very large country,' Detective Sergeant Mill said. 'There are thousands of engineers working in the country, and we don't even know if Dodie and her husband were living in Maidstone at the time the remains of Johnny

Clare were found there. You're trying to make an omelette without any eggs, Sister.'

'It does sound a bit thin,' she admitted.

'On the other hand instinct does count for something. I'll check into the Johnny Clare case first thing tomorrow. If nobody was ever arrested it'll still be on open file. Have you worked out what the written numbers at the side mean?'

'I haven't looked at them again. May I jot them down?'

'Of course. D'ye need a pencil?'

'I have one attached to my little notebook.'

'Do you also carry a knife that takes stones out of horses' hooves?' he enquired dryly.

'I'll provide myself with one,' she promised lightly. 'May I have the numbers please?'

'The first one is ten, dot, eight, dot seventy-five.'

'The tenth of August, 1975?'

'Did anything happen on that date you remember? You'd still have been in college.'

'On vacation. No, I don't recall anything special happening during that vacation.'

'Did you all keep in touch during the vacations?'

'I didn't. I went up home to my family,' Sister Joan said. 'I don't know about the others.'

'The next number is eleven, dot, nine, eighty-four. Wasn't that the date the Clare child disappeared?'

'I'm not sure. It was reported a couple of days later in the newspaper.'

'I'm beginning to recall more details of the case. I was in police college myself at the time, doing my finals.'

Odd, she thought, writing the numbers down to think that he'd been training for his career when she had been training for what she'd hoped would be hers. Well, he'd been more faithful to his ambition than she'd been.

'The next date is sixteen, dot, seven, ninety.'

'The date Johnny Clare's remains were found? Yes, there must be a link! What are the other dates?'

'If they are dates they're not in chronological order. Fifteen, dot, four, seventy-nine. Three, dot, six, seventy-eight. And then five, dot, four, ninety-three.'

'Is that it?'

police coming to the school, of course, to ask questions. He was an adopted child and the police thought that perhaps his real mother had taken him, but she couldn't be traced. After a few years the Clares gave up hope and went back to New Zealand. They'd come from there originally. And then several years later I read in the paper that they'd found him – his remains they called them – buried in a field somewhere.'

'Yes. I heard about it,' Sister Joan said.

'So I'm awfully pleased to hear the little gypsy boy's safe!' Fiona said happily. 'Is this your own pony? Are you allowed to have pets?'

'Not officially, but Lilith was here when the order took over the estate and Alice is being trained to be a guard dog though so far she's a fairly slow learner.'

'This is a lovely place, isn't it?' Fiona looked round with a sweetly wistful expression. 'Not that I'd want to live here! How do you manage without any sex?'

'We sublimate it,' Sister Joan said, her lips quirking. 'Speaking of which – it isn't any of my business but did you really sleep with Bryan?'

'Once or twice.' Fiona looked slightly embarrassed. 'I slept with most people once or twice. I used to hope that I'd fall in love with one of them but I never did.'

'While you were in college or afterwards?'

'Both.' Fiona gave her a questioning look. 'Why are you asking?'

'Not out of idle curiosity,' Sister Joan said. 'Have you heard anyone else speak of Johnny Clare's murder?'

'No, why should they?' Fiona said, puzzled.

'I thought it might have a bearing.'

'On Serge's death, do you mean?' Fiona stopped and considered gravely, then shook her blonde head. 'I didn't know Serge was dead, you know. I was terribly shocked when Barbara came back from the telephone and told us, and now it turns out that she and Paul knew all about it already and never said a word. I can't think why, but then I don't understand any of them any longer. I've been wondering if it was wise to agree to come along to the retreat. At the reunion there were none of them as I remembered them.'

'Not even me?'

They had reached the yard and Sister Joan led Lilith into the stable and began to unsaddle her.

'You haven't really changed,' Fiona said, leaning against the stable door and regarding her speculatively. 'You were always lively and ready for a joke. I heard you went off to live with someone, so I was surprised to find out you were a nun. What happened?'

'I used to think it was the barrier of religion,' Sister Joan said, 'but now I do think that it ended because something better came along.'

'If you say so. It wouldn't suit me personally,' Fiona said with a grimace.

'You went to the States.'

'Oh, I enjoyed myself there!' Fiona said. 'I did some modelling and a bit of acting, and I had one hell of a good time! And I had the sense to get out before I got bogged down in trekking from one casting agent to the next, making guest appearances on third-rate chat shows, all the usual nausea! I came back and started teaching art.'

'You always had good sense,' Sister Joan said, giving Lilith a final pat.

'I'm not clever and I never was a very talented artist,' Fiona said, 'but I'm a survivor.'

'Unlike Sally, Bryan and Serge.'

'That is so weird!' Fiona exclaimed with a little shiver. 'There were ten of us in that photograph and over the last couple of years three of us have died in very odd ways! Don't you think it's peculiar?'

'What do the others think?' Sister Joan evaded as they retraced their footsteps across the cobbled yard towards the enclosure garden.

'I haven't asked them,' Fiona said. 'You know I was rather looking forward to seeing everybody again, and I was quite pleased when I got the photograph. But it hasn't been the way I thought it would be. Barbara's become terribly brittle and businesslike, and Paul—' She stopped, biting her scarlet lip.

'What about Paul?' Sister Joan asked.

'Oh, nothing!' Fiona switched the subject hastily. 'It's not fair to talk about people behind their backs, is it? Anyway after you left the evening sort of soured. Dodie and Paul were bitching at each other and the play wasn't awfully good, and then Barbara was called to the telephone just after we'd started supper and it was you telling her that Serge was dead.'

'Before the play surely?'

'We decided to go on to the play anyway and it wasn't very good, though to be fair I was so upset to hear about Serge that I wouldn't have enjoyed anything even if it was brilliant,' Fiona said. 'After the play we all went home.'

'What time was that?'

'Time?' Fiona looked blank. 'I never know what time it is! About ten-thirty, I think. We had a quick coffee in the bar and agreed to come down here for the retreat and Serena offered to give me a lift. She offered one to Dodie too but Dodie was angling for a lift from Derek, and then Paul came in and said he'd come with them because he has a driving ban – but he drove down to the village last night, didn't he?'

Sister Joan nodded. She was wondering if Fiona was as guileless as she appeared.

'Anyway,' Fiona said, 'I still feel that it was a mistake for us all to meet up again. Isn't there a saying that you can't step into the same river twice?'

'Not unless you run very fast along the bank,' Sister Joan said. 'Fiona, have you any idea who sent the photograph?'

'Not a clue. Does it matter?'

'Whoever sent it wanted us all together down here,' Sister Joan said. 'And whoever that was must have kept track of us all for a long time.'

'And then we all start getting killed off.' Fiona looked uneasy. 'Except that the others died before we got the photograph. Joan – sorry, Sister Joan! did Derek say if Sally's name was on the envelope addressed to him?'

'He didn't mention it, but her death had been reported anyway.'

'I wonder if Bryan got one – I mean I wonder if one was sent to him after he died.'

'If someone's been keeping tabs on us then they'd know Bryan had died too.'

'I suppose.' Fiona reached to pluck a spray of wisteria from the enclosure wall. 'Look, Barbara and Paul say they already knew that Serge was dead, yet they let you go to his flat because they reckoned you'd be curious and get involved – get involved in what? What are you supposed to be finding out?'

'Who killed Johnny Clare?' Sister Joan said.

Fiona's pretty face was a study in perplexity. 'What has that got to do with anything?' she demanded. 'Nobody knew that poor child except me. You're not suggesting that I had anything to do with his death, are you? Oh, surely you can't believe that I'd hurt a child?'

'No, of course not,' Sister Joan said warmly. 'But somebody killed him.'

'But that was ten years ago,' Fiona said. 'I just happened to mention it because of the gypsy child being missing.'

'Serge kept newspaper records of the case,' Sister Joan said.

'Serge wouldn't have done such a thing!' Fiona's cheeks had flushed and her voice rose indignantly. 'I happen to know that Serge was absolutely normal sexually! Absolutely normal! I do think you're clutching at straws, Joan! For heaven's sake we were all friends!'

'Fellow students. And you did say that we'd changed.'

'That's true.' Fiona's temper subsided. 'But Serge wouldn't have hurt anybody. I slept with him several times. He liked girls. And so did Paul!'

'Paul?' Sister Joan paused to look at her.

'He's changed more than any of us!' Fiona said vehemently. 'He used to like girls as much as anyone and, believe me, I'm in a position to know!'

Ten

Lunch had passed smoothly and, as if by common consent, the guests had wandered into the garden, taking advantage of the burst of sunshine that made the autumn day summer again. They lounged in the deck chairs that Sister Perpetua had unearthed – or perhaps lounged wasn't quite the right word for them all, Sister Joan thought, as she paused by the low wall. Serena was certainly stretched out, her ample curves overflowing the sides of the chair, her eyes closed. Serena seemed unconscious of any undercurrents of suspicion. Fiona too appeared to have forgotten her anxieties of earlier in the day and lay supine, her eyes protected by sunglasses, her long legs still tanned golden under her short skirt. Paul and Derek were reading the newspapers she'd brought, Derek reading with a concentrated frown on his dark face and putting each paper down on the folded pile as he finished, Paul scattering newsprint like large pieces of confetti. Dodie had refused a deckchair in favour of a large cushion on which she sat, looking rather like Miss Muffet, her skirts pulled down, a cardigan over her shoulders. She wasn't reading but sat motionless, one hand plucking constantly at the short grass. Near her Barbara, suitably and elegantly attired, in dark-red shirt and matching trousers, her hair coiled behind her head, was sketching on a notepad.

She glanced up, caught Sister Joan's eye, and rose, strolling in an unhurried fashion to the wall.

'Are we supposed to be doing something else?' she enquired.

'It's a free afternoon,' Sister Joan assured her. 'On Sundays we catch up on our spiritual diaries, write letters, read, have our own private devotions – either Father Malone or Father

131

Stephens sometimes drops in for a chat or a visitor may come to the parlour.'

'It sounds very restful,' Barbara said, hooking a long leg over the wall, and joining Sister Joan at the near side. 'I was thinking of taking a walk. Are you allowed to come with me?'

'Yes, of course.'

Was this going to be the confidence she'd been hoping that Barbara would impart? Sister Joan walked on with outward composure and waited.

'I owe you an apology,' Barbara said abruptly when they were out of earshot of the group on the grass.

'Oh?' Sister Joan slowed her pace slightly.

'We wanted to involve you but we didn't know how to go about it,' Barbara said. 'I mean, under normal circumstances, we'd simply have told you what was going on and asked you what you thought we ought to do, but nuns don't get involved in the real world so we had to go about it in a roundabout way.'

'What on earth makes you think that nuns don't live in the real world?' Sister Joan enquired mildly. 'We're not locked up in some rose-coloured boudoir you know.'

'We didn't know,' Barbara said curtly. 'Anyway you dropped out of sight ten years ago. Someone said you'd taken the veil. Then we read an item in the paper about your having helped out in a murder case down here in Cornwall, and it was like fate.'

'Who is "we"?'

'Dodie and I,' Barbara said. 'We've been in touch during the past couple of years. I – met her when I returned from New Zealand and we kept up a casual friendship. Then after Sally was killed and then Bryan died in that hit-and-run incident, we both started thinking.'

'What made you think the two deaths were connected?' Sister Joan asked.

'I had a letter from Sally,' Barbara said, hesitating. 'I'm not sure why she wrote to me. I hadn't run into her more than a couple of times since I got back to England, but she wrote to me. I kept the letter.'

She drew it out of her trouser pocket and passed it over.

They were in the shrubbery that grew thickly above the tennis court. Sister Joan sat down on the top step and unfolded the single sheet of paper.

There was neither date nor address and the writing was uneven as if the writer had composed either in a great hurry or under extreme stress.

Barbara! A very quick note! Could we please meet as soon as possible? I have to talk to somebody very soon. I'll be driving into town next Thursday. Maybe we could have coffee somewhere? If that day doesn't suit you then I'll come again on Friday. No, I'll come into town every afternoon and have coffee at the Casbah Restaurant in Brook Street, between five and six. Come as soon as you can. If I'm not there then something came up and I'll be there the next day. Love Sally.

'What do you think?' Barbara asked. She had remained on her feet, her hands thrust into her pockets.

Sister Joan reread the note, stood up, folded it and handed it back.

'I remember Sally as a very pleasant, placid girl,' she said slowly. 'That letter is a mite muddled, isn't it?'

'You keep it!' Barbara handed it back. 'Frankly it didn't make any sense at all. The point is that I couldn't get into town before the Friday. My firm had sent me up to Chester for a few days to promote a new product and there was no way I could get out of it. I tried phoning her but nobody answered and as she did say in the note she'd try to drive in every day in order to be sure of meeting me I left it until after I got back on the Friday. She didn't turn up and then, after I got back to my flat, Derek phoned in a dreadful state to tell me she was dead.'

'Why did he phone you?'

'Oh, he knew Sally and I met occasionally. He'd tried to phone me that morning but I was still on my way from Chester. I went round to the shop at once. He kept saying that it must have been an accident.'

'Did you tell him about the note?'

'No.' Barbara shook her dark head. 'What was the use? My own theory was that Sally had been in a personal mess of one kind or another and wanted to talk about it. By the Thursday when I still hadn't turned up she became depressed and decided to cut her losses and throw herself out of the car-park. How could I possibly tell him that I thought it possible she'd committed suicide?'

'She'd died on the Thursday?' Sister Joan's fingers tightened slightly on the paper.

'The previous day,' Barbara said. 'On the fourteenth.'

'Of May?'

'Yes.'

'Fourteen, five, ninety-two,' Sister Joan said slowly.

'What?'

'Nothing. Just the date.'

One of those written on the edge of the old newspaper she'd taken from Serge's flat.

'You must have felt very upset,' she said, folding the paper smaller and pushing it deeply into her own pocket. 'Honestly I don't think you ought to blame yourself though. You couldn't help not being there until the Friday and there's not the least proof that Sally committed suicide. Why should she? She'd told you she'd be there every day for the whole week. She wouldn't be very likely to turn up on Monday, Tuesday and Wednesday and then kill herself on the Thursday. I'm sure it was an accident.'

'I hope so,' Barbara said restlessly, 'but I won't ever be certain.'

They had turned and were retracing their steps, veering away from the garden to the other part of the grounds where Sister Martha had, so far, made few inroads.

'When did you get in touch with Dodie again?' Sister Joan broke the silence.

'I had a letter from her,' Barbara said. 'She wrote to me after Bryan died.'

'She knew your address?'

'I ran into her one day after I came back to England. She was in town buying school uniforms for her two kids,' Barbara explained. 'We had a quick coffee and exchanged addresses but I never bothered to contact her again and she didn't contact me until she read about Bryan having been killed by a hit-and-run driver and then she wrote to ask me if I'd heard and wasn't it all very sad? You know Dodie!'

'I'm beginning to think that I never knew any of you

properly,' Sister Joan said wryly. 'Why did Dodie write to you about Bryan?'

'Bryan and I had – something going,' Barbara said. 'I'd been out with him in college, you know – only a few times but then he started seeing Fiona.'

'Sleeping with Fiona.'

'Yes. Yes, sleeping with her. I wasn't prepared to be one of a heap of scalps, so I didn't go out with him again.'

'And, of course, you left in the middle of the second term.'

'To nurse my father, yes.' Barbara met Sister Joan's eyes with a wide look of her own. She was still sticking to her story then. Sister Joan wanted to seize her and shake the truth, whatever it was, out of her, but resisted the impulse. In her own good time Barbara would tell the whole story.

Instead she asked, 'Did Bryan die on the fifth of April last year?'

'Yes. Yes he did. It was in the paper of course.'

Sister Joan forbore mentioning that she hadn't read anything about Bryan Grimes in any newspaper, but had seen the date written on the edge of one of those that Serge had kept. Friendship couldn't be whole and entire without fidelity to the truth, without faithfulness to the memory of what had been shared. She felt a pang of sorrow at the thought that perhaps their friendship had always been a broken and feeble affair.

'And Bryan's death?' She glanced at her taller companion.

'It was a shock,' Barbara said. 'I'd been up to Lincolnshire to see him. He moved back there, you know, after—' She stopped abruptly, turning to twitch a coloured leaf from a tree that leaned out from the hedge.

'After?'

'Oh, nothing.' Barbara crumpled the leaf in her hand, looked at it in distaste and threw it away before striding on so fast that Sister Joan had to scurry to keep up with her.

'So Dodie told you that he'd been killed,' she said. 'You didn't know already?'

'How could I have known?' Barbara said impatiently. 'I'd been up to see him, to talk over old times. Bryan thought it would be nice to remind people of our old plan to hold a reunion on the twentieth anniversary of our first day in college. I agreed and he said he'd arrange it when the time came.'

'He had the photograph?'

'He had the negative,' Barbara said. 'Lord knows why he'd kept it. It was shoved in with a whole heap of other stuff and he said he'd send the copies round in good time. Then I left.'

'And a year after he died we all get copies of the photograph,' Sister Joan said.

'Bryan might have had the photograph and the negative on him when he took that walk,' Barbara said. 'He put them both back into his jacket pocket while I was with him.'

'And you were with him the day before? The night before too?'

'No, just for the day,' Barbara said. 'It was a flying visit from one old friend to another, nothing more. Then Dodie told me that Bryan had been knocked down and killed. I'd mentioned to her that I was going to see him, and she guessed that I wouldn't have heard. I was naturally upset about it, but I didn't think any more about the photograph and then copies of it started to arrive. Derek rang me and said he'd received one, and so did Dodie, and we decided to come along to the reunion and see who else turned up.'

'Knowing that Bryan couldn't have sent them.'

'Someone must've taken them from him, the original and the negative,' Barbara said tensely. 'Don't you see, Joan? Whoever drove a car at him and killed him went through his pockets and found that negative, and had it developed and copies of the group photograph made and then sent them round to us all.'

'Which meant it had to be someone in the photograph who killed him?' Sister Joan shivered slightly.

'That's what Dodie and I figured,' Barbara said.

'You should have gone to the police.'

'With what evidence? Anyway it was more than a year after Bryan's death that the photographs began arriving. That's not evidence of any kind.'

'And you were in the area yourself,' Sister Joan said.

Barbara stared at her and broke into a short laugh. 'You can't honestly think I drove my car at him, went through his pockets and then left him dead or dying in the middle of the road, do you?' she said vehemently. 'Joan, I couldn't do such a thing! Surely you know that much!'

'I just told you: I don't know anything about any of you,'

Sister Joan said. 'You tell me half truths, give me hints, expect me to solve something without having all the facts. I don't know any of you nowadays.'

'I'm still Barbara,' Barbara said.

'Nobody ever changes?' Sister Joan looked at her thoughtfully. 'That's true, I think. You were very quiet and mousy and not really very smart. Underneath are you still like that?'

'You don't pull your punches, do you?' Barbara stared at her and laughed again on a hard, high brittle note.

'And you haven't answered the question.'

'Very well!' Barbara walked on a few paces before she said, crisply, 'I felt stupid and mousy when I was at college because I was intelligent enough to realize fairly quickly that I really didn't have any outstanding talents. I'd end up teaching art in a school somewhere or getting my name at the bottom of greetings cards—'

'Like Fiona and Dodie? They don't mind.'

'They're both good without being great,' Barbara said. 'I wasn't as good as they are and I wanted to be great. I wanted to create something beautiful so badly that I could taste it. I could feel the sweetness of it under my tongue. And every day I looked at my latest effort and wanted to throw it down and stamp on it, smash it into bits. Of course I'd never have dreamed of doing anything of the sort. I was a modest, well-brought-up girl from a middle-class home.'

'So you ran away instead? Left college because you couldn't face competition?'

Barbara had stopped, half turning. To Sister Joan's surprise her face was alight with triumph.

'Ran away!' she echoed. 'Is that what you believe? Oh, Sister dear, you couldn't be more wrong! I—'

Heavy footsteps crashed through the undergrowth as she broke off abruptly. Brother Cuthbert stumbled through, tearing a long trail of sticky creeper from his habit. He looked as if he had run all the way from the old schoolhouse, his face as scarlet as his hair.

'Brother Cuthbert! Are you all right?' Sister Joan took a step forward, and stopped, something cold icing her backbone as she saw his reddened hands.

'I do beg your pardon, Sister – ladies!' He was making a desperate attempt to pull himself together. 'I have had a shock, a really terrible shock!'

'Are you hurt, Brother?'

'No, no.' He lifted his hands, staring at the palms in a kind of sick horror. 'No, not in the least hurt. This is the child's blood. His throat has been cut, you see.'

Inside something was twisting her guts like a vice, but on the surface she knew that her face had merely paled a little. She said, marvelling at the steadiness of her voice, 'Where is the child, Brother Cuthbert?'

'On the moor not far from the convent gates.' He spoke with an effort. 'I was on my way here to ask if there was anything I could do to make the retreat more agreeable for the guests. I stumbled over him. At first I thought he was asleep. Then I saw as I bent to shake his shoulder – I ran here at once. I was going to the kitchen door but I heard voices—'

'Barbara, will you take Brother Cuthbert to the kitchen and get him a good slug of brandy from Sister Perpetua?' Sister Joan said. 'Barbara!'

Barbara turned her head slowly and jerkily as if she were on strings pulled by an inexperienced puppeteer. Her lips were a scarlet slash against greenish-white.

'I can't bear it,' she said, her voice no louder than a whisper. 'I can't bear it.'

'Don't you dare faint or be sick!' Sister Joan said roughly. 'There's no time for that now. Tell Sister Perpetua to ask Mother Dorothy to telephone the police. I shall stay with the child until someone comes.'

'Over to the left about fifty yards beyond the gate,' Brother Cuthbert said. 'God forgive me but I never stopped to say a prayer!'

'Go and get your brandy,' Sister Joan said. 'Go with him, Barbara!'

Leaving them to make their own way to the kitchen she turned and ran towards the main gate.

The body, laid on its back, staring open-eyed at the sky, violated the beauty of the golden afternoon. Some attempt had been made to cover it. Long branches had been laid roughly across it. She must have ridden past earlier without even glancing in that direction. She crouched down, blessing herself, her lips shaping a prayer while her eyes automatically examined the spot.

It had to be the Boswell child. Brown-skinned and lithe in life, grotesque and disjointed in death, with that livid face above the slash of dark red. Near the stiff hand something glittered.

She finished her prayer, bent and picked it up. A tie-pin lay on the palm of her hand, its twisted circle of gold filled with two initials also in gold. C.M. C.M?

She slipped the tie-pin into her pocket and stood up, her eyes moving round the grass that surrounded the small figure. Short, autumn-faded grass, starred with the last of summer's weeds, the branches piled higgledy-piggledy as they must have been disturbed by Brother Cuthbert's large, sandalled feet.

Anyone could have taken the child, killed him, brought him back to the moor near the convent gates. But why bring him so near? The light covering of branches wouldn't have hidden him for long.

She wanted to cover the body, to close the eyes, but the police would be here, and they disapproved of anything being disturbed at the scene of the crime.

Sister Perpetua was hastening through the gates, her freckled face distressed.

'My dear girl, I've brought you a drop of brandy!' she exclaimed. 'Take a good long swallow now.'

'I really don't need it,' Sister Joan protested.

'Have it anyway to oblige me!' Sister Perpetua stepped to the pile of torn branches with their canopy of dying leaves and looked down, her mouth compressed. 'I know the lad,' she said brusquely. 'Nice, friendly child. Used to scrump apples every chance he got. There's the Devil's work in this, Sister.'

'Last evening after the grand silence there were men from the camp looking for him,' Sister Joan said slowly. 'When I rode down into town this morning nobody was about. I assumed the search had been called off. The police hadn't been told.'

'Here they come now.' Sister Perpetua nodded towards the two police cars followed by an ambulance labouring up the track.

'Sisters!' Detective Sergeant Mill acknowledged them briefly and walked over to the body, Constable Petrie at his heels.

'It's young Finn Boswell, sir,' the constable said. 'He'd not been reported missing.'

'We'll get the area cordoned off immediately.' Detective Sergeant Mill was impassive. Whatever his private feelings, and she guessed they were strong since he had two sons of his own, he would set them aside, concentrate on the task in hand.

'Someone ought to go over to the Romany camp,' Sister Joan said.

'Perhaps you ought to go,' Sister Perpetua said unexpectedly. 'They know you and will take it more easily from you than from the police.'

'I'm afraid telling the parents is my job,' Detective Sergeant Mill said, coming over to them. 'On the other hand what Sister Perpetua says makes good sense. Perhaps you could come with me, Sister Joan?'

'You go, Sister. I'll speak to Mother Dorothy,' Sister Perpetua said.

'Very well.' Sister Joan nodded briefly as she turned towards the police car. Time was of the essence in police work, she knew, and she suspected that the boy had probably lain all night beneath the sheltering branches.

'We can talk on the way,' Detective Sergeant Mill said, getting behind the wheel. 'Mother Dorothy rang and gave very brief details. Brother Cuthbert found the lad?'

'Barbara Ford and I were strolling in the grounds when Brother Cuthbert came rushing up,' Sister Joan told him. 'He had walked over to the convent to ask if we needed any help with the retreat, and he stumbled over the boy. I must have ridden past this morning without even noticing.'

'If the body was there then.'

The boy had become a body, another trick to distance himself.

'Someone hid him and then moved him again earlier this morning?'

'We'll find out. Guessing games aren't in my line.' He spoke tensely, his mouth a straight line, but his carefully controlled anger had nothing to do with her. It was anger at the violent death of a young child.

'Sister Perpetua said the Devil had been at work,' she said.

'A human being,' he corrected. 'I've no faith in your Devil,

Sister. A human being, outwardly like you or me, took that little boy, killed him, hid the body—'

'Not very skilfully,' Sister Joan said, frowning. 'The first person out walking would probably have stumbled over it, as Brother Cuthbert did.'

'We'll see.' He swung the car to the right, the track narrowing and twisting as it followed the contours of the moor. Ahead of them a couple of lurcher dogs raised sleepy Sunday heads.

The camp had been there when the Tarquins had been squires of the district and now that the Tarquins had long since gone the brightly painted vardos of the Boswells and Evanses and Lees still stood in their accustomed places. From time to time an official from the local council put in an appearance to shake a head and mutter darkly about lack of sanitation, but the pool of clear water beyond the tip of rusting iron still provided for the clan, and the children whom Sister Joan had taught in the old schoolhouse lounged past with the latest trainer shoes vying with the ancient hoops in their ears.

'If you're here about the fish—!' Padraic Lee appeared from nowhere, trying to smile at Sister Joan, scowl at the detective sergeant, and look innocent all at the same time.

The result was a grimace that twisted his normally pleasant features into the appearance of villainy.

'It's nothing to do with poaching,' Detective Sergeant Mill said. 'You have a Finn Boswell in camp.'

'Hettie Boswell's youngest, yes.'

'You were out on the moor last night looking for him.'

'Aye, for a bit. I spoke to Sister Joan, up near the convent wall. She couldn't answer since it was the silence time.'

'And then you called off the search? You didn't tell the police?' Sister Joan said.

'Weren't no need, Sister. Luther came along and told us the lad was safe. Out doing a bit of mischief like lads will.'

His eyes, black and sharp, moved from one face to the other.

'I'm afraid something has happened, Padraic,' Sister Joan said, glancing at her companion. 'I need to talk to Mrs Boswell.'

'She's over there, building her fire.' Padraic pointed. 'What's happened?'

'We found Finn Boswell,' the detective said, his voice and face carefully neutral.

'Found him?' Padraic stared at them, eyes narrowing.

'He's dead. I'm sorry.'

'Dead? How?'

'He was killed by someone – we don't yet know whom,' Sister Joan said. 'Someone must tell his parents and identify the body later.'

'Killed? Murdered you mean?' Padraic passed a hand over his greasy, greying-black curls. 'But Luther said—'

'We'll need to talk to Luther,' Detective Sergeant Mill said. 'Do you know where he is?'

'Who knows where Luther gets to?' Padraic said. 'I don't understand it. Luther came and told us that Finn was all right. We called off the search. Luther may be a mite addled betimes in the head but he knows the difference between all right and dead!'

Someone had to tell Finn's parents. As Sister Joan looked past the two men towards the caravan where a woman in a flowered overall was bending over a pile of firewood, Padraic said, 'It's best if the sergeant gives the news, Sister. They'd want it official as if they were important like.'

'Yes. I understand.' Sister Joan nodded and turned back towards the car. In life little Finn Boswell had been one among many. In death he assumed stature which his parents would wish to dignify with an official announcement.

She was too restless to sit in the car and so walked past it, her eyes lowered because when one was in a state of turmoil it was a shield to keep custody of the eyes in approved conventual style.

One of the guests at the retreat had killed Finn Boswell, just as they had killed Patricia Mayne, and Bryan Grimes, and possibly Sally and Serge too. Five deaths that had to be connected somehow. Six deaths! She had forgotten momentarily about Johnny Clare. One thread connected them all. She took the tie-pin out of her pocket and looked at the glittering initials. It was her clear duty to hand it over to the police. Of course she would do so. But her fidelity to her old friends wasn't some chimera to be wiped off the mirror of her mind. First she had a few questions to ask. Old friends deserved the chance to offer an explanation at least.

'Sister! You need more apples picking?'

Luther had loped from behind one of the heaps of firewood piled about the straggle of caravans and trailers.

'Not today, Luther.' She repressed a slight start. 'Today is Sunday.'

'Sunday.' He considered the word for a moment, then nodded. 'No poaching on Sunday,' he said virtuously. 'I telled Finn.'

'You told Finn not to go poaching?'

There was no use in displaying the least flicker of excitement because Luther was apt to take fright and vanish.

'Last night,' he said. 'We were looking for him. All the men seeking on the moor. I gave them the message.'

'From Finn?'

'From Finn and his friend,' Luther said. 'Finn said he going to the convent with his friend to see the sisters and he'd come home after breakfast. I was to tell that to his mam so she'd not fret.'

'Finn was with a friend?'

Luther nodded.

'Did the friend speak to you?'

Luther shook his head.

'You said you had a message from both of them?'

'Finn spoke for his friend,' Luther said, obviously cudgelling his memory. 'Finn said his friend had the toothache. It's nasty is the toothache. I had a toothache once and Mama Sarah gave me cloves to burn out the pain and—'

'What did Finn's friend look like?'

She had spoken too vehemently. Luther's face had gone blank, only his eyes shifting.

'I've not done nothing wrong,' he said uneasily.

'No, of course you haven't,' Sister Joan reassured. 'You've remembered the message very cleverly. Was Finn's friend a little boy?'

'No, Sister!' Luther spoke with a sudden flare of energy. 'It'd not be right to leave two young 'uns out at night! He was a man grown, but he'd a scarf round his mouth for the toothache.'

'And Finn said?'

' "Tell Mam I'm going up to the sisters and will come home after breakfast." Then he said, "Come on, Colin",' Luther said, in the singsong tones of remembering, 'And then they went away into the dark.'

Eleven

'I'll run you back to the convent, Sister,' Detective Sergeant Mill said as she rejoined him.

Within the caravan from which he had just emerged she could hear the high-pitched keening of grief. To have offered to give comfort would have been an impertinence.

In the car he sat for a moment in silence before starting the engine. Another police car had driven up and two constables were preparing to take statements from the group of Romanies who had congregated, the women wailing, the men hard-eyed. It would be better for the killer if the police caught him first.

'What did Luther have to say to you?' he asked abruptly.

'You saw him?'

'Ducking away as I came out of the Boswell vardo. You wouldn't be holding back any information in the mistaken belief that you owed some kind of faithfulness to your old friends, would you?'

'I have one or two questions to ask first and then I'll have some useful information, I hope. Can you give me a little time?' she asked.

'Officially I can't give you any time at all,' he said. 'Unofficially I shall give you until tomorrow morning. By then we'll have the preliminary pathologist's report, statements from the lad's people. I'll come over at ten to have a few words with the guests at the retreat. If anyone suddenly decides to leave call me. I'll be at the station.'

'Thank you,' she said soberly.

'It has to be one of the guests.' He spoke broodingly, following his own train of thought. 'Johnny Clare, Patricia Mayne and now Finn Boswell all had their throats cut. There's a link. Has to be!'

'I'll find out what I can.'

They had reached the convent gates where he slowed and stopped. At a little distance a yellow tarpaulin flapped in the breeze over the pile of branches. The ambulance had gone. Constable Petrie was talking to a man with a camera.

'Be very careful, Sister.' Detective Sergeant Mill spoke without taking his eyes from the driving mirror. 'I'm bending the rules for you.'

'I appreciate it.' She threw him a swift smile as she got out of the car, and walked at a brisk pace through the gates without looking back. In her pocket the tie-pin felt red hot.

Sister Perpetua met her at the back door.

'Brother Cuthbert borrowed the van and went off to find Father Malone,' she said. 'They'll both be giving what comfort they can, though that's precious little compared with the death of a child. Miss Ford insisted she was all right and went off to the postulancy to lie down for a bit. The others are still in the garden. I'm afraid it wasn't possible to keep the news from them. They'd heard the police cars and the two gentlemen walked down to the gates to have a look.'

'Thank you, Sister.' Sister Joan crossed the yard again and took the path that led between the high shrubbery to the tennis court.

Barbara wasn't lying down. She was pacing the court, hands thrust in her pockets, her head bent. She swung round as Sister Joan reached the steps and stared up at her.

'What happens now?' she demanded. 'Do we all get grilled by the police or what?'

'Only by me,' Sister Joan said mildly, seating herself on the top step. 'You were Johnny Clare's mother, weren't you?'

A flash of time lengthened into a long moment. Then Barbara sat down on the lowest step, twisting herself sideways with her back against a stray piece of fencing.

'How did you find out?' she asked.

'An intelligent guess. You left college halfway through the second term because your father was sick? Then he recovered, remarried his nurse and you all three emigrated to New Zealand? Your father was killed in a gliding accident in the year he was supposed to be recovering from a serious illness. So you left for another reason. The only one I could think of was pregnancy. Twenty years back we didn't take such things as lightly as people do today. And you were quiet, rather shy. You didn't sleep around.'

'Johnny was born in New Zealand on the tenth of August, 1975,' Barbara said tonelessly. 'Dad had been killed a couple of months before and I had no family except for a cousin in New Zealand who invited me to join her. So I went.'

Another of the dates written on the old newspaper was clarified.

'And Johnny was adopted out there?' she asked.

'Not through an official adoption agency,' Barbara said. 'The Clares were neighbours of my cousin and they offered to take him. Henry Clare was an engineer and he and his wife could provide a loving, stable home for a child, so I was glad to agree.'

'He didn't know you were his mother?'

Barbara shook her head.

'They told him he'd been specially chosen – you know, the way people do. In the summer of seventy-eight, just before Johnny's birthday, they came over to England.'

'On the third of June, 1978,' Sister Joan murmured.

'Somewhere around that time,' Barbara said. 'Why?'

'Serge left a pile of old newspapers in his flat,' Sister Joan said. 'He'd written some dates down the margin of one.'

'Then he did have—' Barbara broke off abruptly, pulling up a tuft of grass and turning it over and over in her hand.

'Was Serge collecting dates – evidence of some kind?' Sister Joan asked.

'Evidence, yes. I wasn't sure what proof he had,' Barbara said. 'He never would say.'

'Proof as to who murdered Johnny?'

'He had theories,' Barbara said, throwing the grass away and dusting her hand over her trousers. 'Serge loved mysteries.'

'Was Serge the father?'

'Serge? No, not Serge.' Barbara gave a dismal little laugh. 'Serge was handsome. He could have any girl he chose. It wasn't unlikely he'd have looked twice at mousy old me! No, Bryan was the father.'

'You and Bryan?' Sister Joan shook her head slightly. 'I didn't know you even dated.'

'We didn't,' Barbara said wryly. 'The truth is that Bryan was shy with girls. He was more at ease with his own sex. But we got stuck together at the Christmas party, and everybody else was pairing off or going on somewhere, and one thing led to another. You know what it's like!'

'If I remember rightly I spent that particular Christmas being bored to death by a second-year student who believed he was the reincarnation of Gauguin,' Sister Joan said. 'Did Bryan know about the baby?'

'I didn't tell him,' Barbara said. 'At least not at first. We weren't in a position to get married and Bryan was a nice person. He'd have fretted. I figured it was my own problem. My dad was very supportive, but then Dad was killed in the flying accident and Phyllis, my cousin, invited me to stay with her.'

'When did you tell Bryan?' Sister Joan asked.

'I wrote to him,' Barbara said. 'The Clares had kept in touch and I wrote to Bryan, to tell him that I'd had a child. All right, so it was a silly thing to do! Johnny had been adopted, so why tell Bryan about something that was over and done? I don't know why – impulse, I suppose! Anyway he wrote back, asking me about Johnny. It was a nice letter. He seemed interested – not just in the fact that I'd had a baby but in me personally!'

'You thought you might get together?'

'Pathetic, isn't it?' Barbara grinned ruefully. 'Eight years after I'd had our child adopted I wrote to tell him all about it, when it was too late for him to do anything at all. He wrote back – such a nice letter, asking me all about Johnny. I hadn't seen Johnny for years but the Clares kept in touch and I told Bryan everything I knew. There was never any idea of claiming him back, but it was nice to be able to tell him that he'd fathered such a nice, bright little boy.'

'And then Johnny was murdered,' Sister Joan said.

'I was never brought into the case at all,' Barbara said. 'The adoption had taken place in New Zealand. There was no reason to connect me with Johnny and the Clares said nothing. Anyway in the beginning he simply vanished. Someone who wanted a child might've taken him.'

'Bryan?'

'No, Bryan didn't want to settle down with anything resembling a family. At heart he was a loner, and the Clares knew that I was making a good career for myself. My life has no room for a child in it. I've worked on my image, got rid of my mousiness.'

'Very effectively,' Sister Joan said. 'I hardly recognized you.'

'They found Johnny's remains six years later.' Barbara's voice had sharpened, speeded up as if she wanted to reach the end. 'In a field outside Maidstone.'

'Where Dodie lives.'

'Where Dodie lives,' Barbara repeated tonelessly. 'Dodie and I were in contact again, and when I read in the newspaper – I confided in her about my having had a child and who the father was and what had happened. She was very sweet to me, very sympathetic indeed. She has two adopted children herself so she knows—'

'Dodie's children are adopted?'

'Yes. Hasn't she told you?' Barbara bit her lip. 'Look, don't say anything! She likes to pretend that they're her own natural children. They were adopted in the usual way. I met them once. Nice children.'

'And you tried to find out who'd killed Johnny?'

'No, why should we?' Barbara said. 'I thought it was one of those random murders, some crazy pervert. You read about them in the papers all the time. Sooner or later they're caught and tried and locked up at the taxpayers' expense for psychiatrists to examine. I thought it was someone like that.'

'And then?' Sister Joan sat very still.

'Then a couple of years after Johnny's body had been found I had the note from Sally, saying she wanted to meet me in town. It was obvious she had something on her mind.'

'Did Sally know you were Johnny's real mother?'

'I don't know. I never said anything to her, but Dodie may have done. They saw each other occasionally.'

'And Sally fell out of the top storey of a multistorey car-park,' Sister Joan said.

'Before she'd had the chance to tell me what was on her mind.' Barbara rubbed her forehead with her clenched fist. 'Derek rang me and told me what had happened. He was distraught, really shattered. He really loved Sally. They'd been happy. He was dependent on her for all the practical things.'

'Did he know she was coming to meet you?'

'I don't know. I didn't mention it. I mean he knew we met now and then.'

'It could have been an accident,' Sister Joan said consideringly. 'There were two witnesses in the street below who saw her fall and said she was quite alone.'

'As far as they could tell,' Barbara said impatiently. 'Look, there were boards up at the aperture with warning notices on them. Not fixed boards so it was possible to step round them and lean out. There could have been someone there.'

'And then Bryan was killed.' Sister Joan rose and began pacing herself, her face sombre.

'We wanted to remind everybody of the reunion,' Barbara said, joining her. 'We hoped that when we were all together again someone might shed some light on why Sally died, on what happened to Johnny—'

'You thought it was someone crazy.'

'We thought Dodie might know something,' Barbara said.

'Dodie! Dodie wouldn't—'

'No, of course not! But Johnny's remains were found within a quarter of a mile of Dodie's house, and there's something else.' Barbara paused, biting her lip.

'You may as well tell me,' Sister Joan said.

'Henry Clare was – still is – an engineer. Dodie's husband is an engineer too. They'd actually met. When Dodie contacted me she said that she felt dreadful about what had happened to Johnny because her husband, Colin, had met Henry Clare on business on several occasions. She thought it was a strange coincidence.'

'And you and Bryan thought it might be something more?'

'We didn't know!' Barbara spoke with a kind of dreary ferocity. 'We simply didn't know!'

'And then Bryan was knocked down and killed.'

'And the negative of the group photograph taken from his pocket. At least I don't know that for certain but it's the only thing that makes sense!'

'And where did Serge fit into all this?'

'He went to Bryan's funeral,' Barbara said. 'I went out for a meal with him afterwards and we talked. I told him about Johnny and Johnny's death and Sally's death, and it seemed to us both there was a link. Serge said that he'd do a little ferreting around and after that we parted company.'

'You kept in touch?'

'From time to time. Serge said that he was trying to build up a case. He said that if we found some evidence we ought to bring you in on it. He'd read somewhere that you'd solved a case involving the murder of a child down here in Cornwall.'

'And then Serge apparently committed suicide and you and Paul Vance decided to trick me into meeting you!'

'It wasn't like that!' Barbara protested. 'Look, you're a nun now and you wouldn't have been allowed to volunteer any help. We were trying to think of some excuse to contact you when the photographs started arriving. Bryan couldn't have sent them.'

'And neither could Sally or Serge,' Sister Joan said. 'Fiona? She teaches art at Johnny's old school.'

'Fiona does?' Barbara stopped dead, staring down at her shorter companion. 'She never said.'

'You hadn't been in contact with her?'

'I don't think any of us had seen her or heard from her in years. When she turned up at the reunion I was surprised.'

'She happened to mention that she'd been teaching at a school from where a little boy called Johnny Clare disappeared when we were discussing what might have happened to Finn Boswell. Fiona was worried about him and I – I reassured her that the search had been called off so I reckoned he was safe.'

'Do you think whoever killed Johnny killed the gypsy boy too?' Barbara asked.

Unconsciously Sister Joan's hand strayed into her pocket where the tie-pin lay with its betraying initials of C.M.

'What about Serena?' she evaded.

'Serena doesn't know anything about anything,' Barbara said. 'All Serena cares about is getting through life as easily as possible with the help of Daddy's fortune.'

'Derek? Is he in on this "building up a case" scheme?'

'We thought about it,' Barbara said, 'but when I tried to talk to him after Sally was killed he told me that we were just making fools of ourselves. That if we thought there was anything suspicious about her death then we ought to go to the police. He had no idea she'd arranged to meet me.'

'Does he know that you were Johnny Clare's mother?'

'I'm sure he doesn't. I didn't even tell Sally about that. Why should I?' They had reached the low wall that bounded the postulancy and she turned, spreading her hands palms upward in a gesture of defeat.

'The more I try to sort things out the more confused I become,' she said. 'Bryan and I slept together once and I had a child and gave him up for adoption and made a whole new life for myself. I made a whole new personality for myself. Bright, smart, successful career girl. And now it's all unravelling. I'm unravelling, Joan, and I don't think I can take very much more.'

'You were sick when I told you that Serge's friend had had her throat cut,' Sister Joan said, inexorably.

'What else did you expect?' Barbara demanded. 'It was one death too many! Johnny had his throat cut! My own child – and Sally fell from a great height and Bryan was left dying or dead in the road, and someone gave Serge an overdose of drugs—'

'You can't be sure of that.'

'Of course I'm sure!' Barbara cried. 'Listen! Serge rang me up when he got the photo reminding us of the reunion. He knew it wasn't Bryan who'd sent them round because Bryan was dead. He had a theory that whoever had sent them was teasing us in a horrible way, saying that mocked all our old bonds of friendship! He said that he was building up a case.'

'And where did Patricia Mayne fit in?'

'Maybe he talked to her,' Barbara said wearily. 'Maybe he tried out his ideas on her. How do I know?'

From the other side of the tennis court Paul called, 'Can anyone tell me what's going on? There's a damned great tarpaulin stretched beyond the main gate and sundry rural policemen prowling about, looking for clues, I daresay!'

'I don't know what's happening,' Sister Joan called back, moderating her tone as he loped nearer. 'I'm a nun, not a detective!'

'But the kid's dead?'

'Very dead,' Sister Joan said coldly.

Paul shrugged. 'It's ruined Sunday afternoon,' he drawled.

'You're offensive!' Barbara said tightly. 'Everything's just a game to you, isn't it? Something that might or might not make a good television programme!'

'*Chacun à son goût!*' Paul said lightly. 'Well, Sister dear, have you solved the mystery yet?'

'Almost.' Drawing herself up and lifting her chin, she answered him coolly. 'There are one or two points to clarify, a couple of things to slot into place. Soon I'll have the complete picture.'

'Are you serious?' The laughter in his eyes had died, quenched like a flame.

'Never more so,' she said. 'Excuse me, but I have to go over to the main house. Sister Teresa and Sister Marie are preparing supper and though they wouldn't ask they'd appreciate an offer of help.'

She went past him, lifting her hand to Barbara in a small gesture of dismissal. Inside she could feel anger rising. Anger that they'd involved her in something without giving her the opportunity to refuse, anger that she was still being presented with a distorted picture, anger above all that one person was watching and smiling because she had been manipulated through old bonds of fidelity to her fellow students into playing a sick and macabre game.

Fiona and Serena were still with Derek in the garden, the three of them in deck chairs, heads together, absorbed in murmured conversation. No doubt trying to work out who'd committed the murder, she thought sourly, as if violent death were one of the activities laid on for the retreat. None of them looked up as she went by.

'Sister Joan!'

Mother Dorothy had come out into the grounds and was looking round.

'Yes, Reverend Mother?' Sister Joan reached her superior's side.

'I'd be grateful,' Mother Dorothy said, with nicely controlled asperity, 'if you'd kindly tell me what's happening. You went to the camp with Detective Sergeant Mill?'

'Yes, Mother. Sister Perpetua advised it. We both thought that you would have advised such a course of action too.'

'It is never wise,' Mother Dorothy said, 'to try to read the mind of a prioress. However in this instance you were perfectly correct. Were you able to give any comfort?'

'It would've been an impertinence to try,' Sister Joan said

soberly.

'You spoke to me before of certain matters connected with your former friends that troubled you,' Mother Dorothy said, beginning to walk with her round to the front of the building. 'Does the death of this unfortunate child have any bearing?'

'It's another part of the same puzzle,' Sister Joan said.

'You are, I hope, not holding back any information from the police?'

Mother Dorothy's eyes behind the steel-rimmed spectacles were disconcertingly shrewd.

'I have pieces of information from all over the place,' Sister Joan confided. 'I made it clear to Detective Sergeant Mill that I would be laying that information before him tomorrow morning. He was good enough to allow me that space of time. Would you tell them all that at supper tonight?'

There was a heartbeat of silence. Then Mother Dorothy said, mildly enough, 'Why hold back?'

'Because these people were in college with me and some of them are relying on me to help them. I owe them a certain fidelity.'

'Fidelity is always bound up with truth, isn't it?' Mother Dorothy said. 'If we are faithful to the truth then we cannot betray ourselves, and to be true to oneself is the highest fidelity.'

'Surely fidelity to God?' Sister Joan said.

'At the deepest level isn't it the same thing?' Mother Dorothy gave her a kindly glance.

'I have to talk to someone, find out something else first,' Sister Joan said. 'I also ought to offer some help in the kitchen.'

'Pray don't!' Mother Dorothy said quickly. 'Since Sister Teresa and Sister Marie took over the cooking the meals have been excellent. You said you wished to talk to someone?'

'To Dodie Mason – Dorothy Mason.'

'My namesake.' The prioress gave a wry little smile. 'I am infinitely grateful to my own parents that they never shortened my name. No woman of forty ought to go round answering to the name of Dodie! She went into the chapel a few minutes ago. May I suggest that you simply go in and sit down there? Other people's prayers are not to be lightly intruded upon.'

'Thank you, Reverend Mother.'

She walked rapidly towards the front door, turned into the chapel passage and slowed her pace. It would avail her nothing if she rushed in like a bull in a china shop.

Dodie sat in one of the pews, her hands in her lap, a scarf over her head. She turned slightly as Sister Joan came in and nodded a greeting, speaking in a loud whisper as the latter genuflected before the altar.

'I hope it's all right? My not being a Catholic? I just felt like a bit of peace and quiet. There's been another murder, hasn't there?'

'Another murder?'

'Sister Joan sat down next to her but not too close.

'Ten years ago,' Dodie said in the same half whisper. 'A little boy called Johnny Clare was killed and his remains found years later quite near to where we lived. I feel as if everything is happening all over again but somehow in an upside down kind of way. As if I were in a play with all the lines being said backwards.'

'Your children are adopted,' Sister Joan said. 'Couldn't you have—'

'Oh, I don't think there's anything wrong with me,' Dodie said. 'I'm not certain, of course.'

'But you've been married fifteen years,' Sister Joan said, 'Surely by now—?'

'Not when I'm still a virgin,' Dodie said.

'Still a—' Sister Joan tried to grasp at reality for a moment. What she was hearing simply couldn't be, didn't make sense.

'Colin would never consummate the marriage,' Dodie said. 'Never.'

'I don't understand. Why marry you if—?'

'He needed a wife and children to help his chances of promotion,' Dodie said calmly, as if she were reading a shopping list. 'Of course I didn't know that when I married him. I thought he respected me too much to sleep with me before the ceremony and after that – I stayed on. My family would have been horrified, pitying. I had my pride.'

'But why?'

'Why didn't he?' Dodie gave a little shiver. 'He liked men – boys, you see. Not that anyone would have guessed. He was always very careful. And it didn't happen very often. After it happened he'd – when you came into my room last night you saw the bruises. They're old ones. It isn't a regular occurrence.'

'You could have the marriage annulled.'

'My children are mine even if they are adopted,' Dodie said. 'They go to a very good school. I'd not shame them.'

Sister Joan put her hand in her pocket and drew out the tie-pin.

'This was by the body of Finn Boswell, the gypsy child,' she said. 'The C.M. is for Colin Mason, isn't it? Do you understand what this means, Dodie?'

'That Colin killed the little boy?' Dodie looked at the glinting circle almost with indifference. 'No, he helped bury the first one I think, but he didn't kill the gypsy boy. You're on the wrong track there. Entirely on the wrong track. Excuse me.'

Rising, bobbing her head vaguely in the direction of the altar, she turned and went neatly and swiftly out of the chapel.

'How do you know?' Barbara demanded. 'We might have seen something and not known whether it was important or not.'

'Do we know when the little boy was killed?' Fiona asked.

'Yesterday afternoon,' Sister Joan said. 'He wasn't missed until after dark.'

'Bit careless of his parents, wasn't it?' Paul said.

'The Romany children are brought up to be self-reliant,' Sister Joan said. 'Anyway there's very little crime round here. Children can still play out on the moors in comparative safety.'

'Does that mean the police think that we might have done it?' Serena looked uneasy.

'That's a perfectly horrid idea!' Fiona shuddered.

'You and I came down together,' Serena said.

'And Paul and Derek came down with me,' Dodie reminded them.

'I came by train. Joan met me at the station,' Barbara said.

'But after we all arrived here we did quite a lot of wandering around,' Fiona said brightly.

'What were you all doing while Sister Joan was meeting me?' Barbara asked.

'I was unpacking,' Serena said. 'It took a long time to fit everything in. They don't provide much cupboard space in convents.'

'Nuns don't have such an enormous wardrobe,' Fiona said. 'I was unpacking too and then I went for a little walk round. I didn't go very far.'

'I walked over to the chapel,' Dodie said. 'There were a couple of nuns there praying and I didn't like to disturb them so I came back and started clearing away the cups and saucers.'

'I took a stroll round the grounds,' Paul volunteered. 'I saw Derek doing his Tarzan act up a tree on my way back.'

'Helping that little nun with the apple picking,' Derek nodded.

'Yes. I saw you there.' Sister Joan sat down by the table and drummed her fingers lightly on its polished pine surface.

'After that we were all together and we went over to the big house for supper,' Serena said. 'Anyway this is just silly! I can't believe that one of us grabbed a child, killed him, and then walked back here in time for supper!'

'Since we're all strangers here then it's only natural the police will want to check us out,' Derek said.

'Well, I don't want to talk about it any longer,' Fiona said. 'This is supposed to be a pleasant social hour for heaven's sake! Let's play a game or something.'

'Murder?' Paul suggested.

'I don't understand you!' Fiona stared at him accusingly. 'You used to be so nice and normal and now – now I don't know you at all! I don't know any of you!'

'Let's have a quiz or something,' Serena said with desperate gaiety.

'Who killed Finn whatever his name was?' Paul said.

'I'm going for a walk!' Dodie was on her feet, her rather prissy personality seeming to disintegrate, to be submerged by something else.

'I have to check up on Alice and Lilith anyway,' Sister Joan said. 'If anyone wants me after chapel I'll be in the stable.'

'Hoping for a confession before the police arrive?' Barbara said sharply.

'Oh, confession or not,' Sister Joan said calmly, her insides jerking, 'I think I've just about worked everything out now.'

'You do believe me, don't you?' Dodie said as they went out together. 'Colin never killed anybody. He's not a murderer whatever else he might be. You won't tell the police about the tie-pin you found?'

'It's against the law to withhold evidence,' Sister Joan said.

'But surely you owe something to your old friends?'

They were crossing the dark tennis court and a gust of wind caught them both, whirling dead leaves in its wake, lifting the hem of Sister Joan's habit, spiralling through Dodie's neat, greying curls.

'Old friends?' Sister Joan heard the snap of irritation in her own voice. 'Old friends who don't contact me for years and then decide to involve me in something about which I know nothing! That isn't friendship: that's exploitation!'

'Colin didn't do it,' Dodie repeated. 'He couldn't have done it!'

'Why not?' They had reached the steps and she stopped and turned, her voice low and vehement. 'Colin likes little boys, doesn't he? He never consummated the marriage with you!

Did you know about his sexual tastes before you adopted the children?'

'No, of course not! I thought he had – difficulties but I never knew that!' Dodie exclaimed.

'Otherwise you'd not have risked adopting children? Is that why they're in boarding-school? Is that why you stay with him?'

'He'd never have hurt our own children,' Dodie said defensively, 'but one can never be sure. I felt I ought to stay.'

'What happened ten years ago?' Sister Joan demanded. 'Something did.'

'Colin was on a big work project,' Dodie said. 'He was working on it with a man called Henry Clare. He and his wife came to dinner once. They were nice people. They talked about their adopted son quite a lot. They were proud of him. I talked about our two. Simon was two and Cecily was four months old. Her adoption had just gone through. I remember they talked about all the tests they'd taken and I had to sit there, nodding and agreeing as if I'd taken the same tests myself, and all the time wanting to say – our situation isn't like yours. My husband has never slept with me. But, of course, I served coffee and chatted and envied them, because it was clear Henry Clare loved his wife, and I said nothing. I said nothing.'

'And then their child disappeared,' Sister Joan said.

'A few weeks later. Colin came home from work and told me. He seemed genuinely sorry. I think he was sorry.'

'Because he'd killed Johnny Clare?'

'No!' Dodie said, nervously defiant as they reached the shallow steps. 'No, Colin wasn't like that! He was sick – it is a sickness, isn't it? He used to knock me about from time to time and one day he told me that he was really punishing himself for what he did. He begged me to stay with him, not to leave or tell anybody. He said he'd get treatment.'

'When did he confess that?'

'When Johnny Clare's body was found,' Dodie said. 'Honestly, he didn't mention that had made him confide in me, but I guessed it. I guessed he'd had something to do with it – not the actual killing but helping to bury the body perhaps. The Clares had given up hope and gone back to New Zealand, and there was no way that Johnny could've been brought back to life! And then there were the children, my children! How could I possibly bring them into it – all the publicity and the – so I said nothing.'

'And then Sally died?'

'I read about that,' Dodie said. 'I wrote to Derek to tell him how sorry I was.'

'He seems to be pretty devastated by it still,' Sister Joan said.

'He couldn't believe that it'd been an accident,' Dodie said tensely. 'He wrote back, thanking me for my letter, saying that he thought Sally might have been having an affair or something and had committed suicide because she was unhappy.'

'And then what?'

'Then I – oh, what's that?' Dodie had stopped dead again, her small, trim figure poised as if for flight.

Ahead of them where the shrubbery petered out into rough grass that bordered the low wall of the enclosure gardens there were discs of light spraying the ground and voices.

'Sister Joan, is that you?'

Detective Sergeant Mill strode forward, lowering his torch. 'Who's with you?'

'Dodie – Mrs Mason.' Sister Joan, for the first time in their acquaintanceship, wished he had delayed his arrival for a few minutes. At her side she could feel Dodie shrink into silence again.

'Dorothy Mason.' He sounded quiet and formal, his voice devoid of feeling. 'I'm here to arrest you for the murder of your husband, Colin Mason. You don't have to say anything but what you do say will—'

His words beat against the rising wind. At her side Dodie gave a little cry as if she had just pricked her finger on something.

'Detective Sergeant Mill, is there anything I can do?' Sister Joan asked. 'Dodie has the right to a lawyer.'

'Oh, I don't mind telling you,' Dodie said. 'I couldn't take the beatings any longer, you see, and I couldn't go on pretending that we lived a neat, normal little life. I put a massive dose of sleeping powders in his nightcap just before we came down here.'

'On Friday night?' Detective Sergeant Mill said.

'Was it Friday? Yes, I believe it was,' Dodie said. 'He never woke up again. I packed my case and took a bus to where I'd arranged to meet Derek and Paul to come down here. I suppose it doesn't matter now if you give the police the tie-pin, Joan.'

'It's here.' Sister Joan took it out of her pocket.

'You see it wasn't Colin who killed the little Boswell boy,' Dodie said. 'Colin had been dead for ages by the time that happened.'

'You'll have to come down to the station, Mrs Mason. We'll provide a solicitor for you,' Detective Sergeant Mill said.

'Oh, I don't mind making a statement,' Dodie said. 'It'll be a relief in a way.'

Constable Petrie had stepped forward to take her arm. In the torchlight his young face looked embarrassed, as if escorting a woman to the police car interfered with his rosy vision of ladies.

'Don't worry.' Detective Sergeant Mill's voice warmed slightly as he looked at Sister Joan. 'We tried to contact Colin Mason and were informed his body had just been found. Obviously his wife left the tie-pin by the body in the hope of incriminating her husband. It was bad luck for her that the body was found and the time of death so firmly established. We'll ask for a good local solicitor and make no objection to bail.'

He turned away and went towards his car, leaving her standing there in the half dark.

She felt cold and sick. If Dodie had only had the courage to seek help years before, to take her children and herself to some place of safety and to forget her suburban pride, so much pain might have been averted.

Footsteps pounded across the rough ground before the steps. Barbara called, 'Are you both all right? We don't think anyone ought to go wandering about alone!'

'Where's Dodie?' Derek, keeping pace with Barbara, stopped to look round.

'I thought I heard a car!' Fiona, slowed down by her high heels, was bringing up the rear.

'The police came,' Sister Joan said.

'Where's Dodie?' Fiona had caught them up and stood, clutching a flimsy jacket round her.

'The police came,' Sister Joan said numbly. 'She's gone to make a statement.'

'Dodie?!' Fiona's voice emerged as a small squeak.

'She'll not say one word about her husband,' Derek said gloomily. 'She'll alibi him until the end of time.'

'They can't think that Dodie had anything to do with anything!' Barbara said. 'You ought to have stopped them, Joan.'

'For heaven's sake!' Sister Joan said irritably. 'I can't tell the police what to do! You must think nuns have some special power denied to ordinary citizens!'

'I don't know about the rest of you,' Derek said, 'but I feel like a stiff drink. This place is getting on my nerves. Fiona? Barbara?'

'Good idea,' Fiona said promptly.

'Joan?' Barbara gave her a questioning look.

'It's nearly time for chapel,' Sister Joan said. 'You three go – and don't get any ideas about storming the police station to rescue Dodie.'

They went past her, Derek with an arm protectively about each of the two women. That left Paul with Serena. She turned abruptly and retraced her steps, hurrying across the rough ground, down the steps again and across the old tennis court. It was irrational but she needed to be sure.

The front door of the postulancy was ajar. She entered the narrow hallway quietly, hearing a murmur from the recreation-room. Surely they weren't settling down to a peaceful game of Scrabble, unaware of the conflicting emotions dizzying the mind!

They weren't playing Scrabble. At the door Sister Joan paused, instinctively holding her breath. Not that it would have mattered if she'd arrived with trumpets and a band, she thought, staring at the two interlocked figures. Unclothed they might have posed for a sculpture representing 'The lovers'.

She turned and went out again, leaving the front door open, her own mind swirling with thoughts. Plump, lazy, good-natured Serena either had the power to effect an amazing conversion in Paul Vance's sexual make-up or she had been missing something all along!

She was going to be late for chapel. She hastened her pace, almost running by the time she reached the main house.

The others were coming down by the main staircase from

their hour of recreation. She drew a deep breath, composed her face to bland sweetness, lowered her eyes, and fell in with the others.

In the chapel there was usually peace even when the world outside pressed down upon one's spirits. Genuflecting, kneeling in her accustomed place, her fingers lightly clasping the rosary at her belt, her lips moving in the familiar recitation, she was outwardly indistinguishable from her companions.

Where had it all begun? Ten youngsters coming together to study art, each one with hopes and dreams, each one with a private space into which they allowed only a few.

Think of them as they were! Think!

Serena had been lazy and untidy, coasting through life on her father's money. Paul had been pleasant and ambitious and – normal. Paul had been normal. Paul, she thought suddenly, had been heterosexual all along! So for some purpose of his own he had elected to – she believed the phrase was 'camp it up'. These days every shade of sexuality was regarded as 'normal'. Twenty years before matters were different. 'Coming out of the closet' required real courage. Barbara and Bryan had had a fleeting affair and Barbara had fled to New Zealand to bear her child. Johnny Clare, adopted by the Clares who couldn't have children of their own, nice people who'd kept in touch with Barbara. Henry Clare had worked with Dodie's husband, with Colin Mason who'd hankered after small boys. And Colin Mason, hearing about the Clares' little boy, had lured him away and killed him – no, Dodie had insisted that her husband would stop short of killing and, in any case, Colin Mason couldn't have killed Finn Boswell. Whoever had killed Finn had given his name as Colin and Luther had heard it, had seen the man, his face muffled in a scarf 'for the toothache'. Someone had said something recently. Someone had said something that didn't fit.

They were on the third decade of the Mysteries and she hadn't paid the smallest attention. Faithfulness to one's former comrades ought not to supersede fidelity to the spiritual life she was vowed to follow. She wrenched her attention back to the words and the spirit of the words, the stained-glass images of the ancient story flowing into her mind.

'As it was in the beginning, is now and ever shall be, amen.' Mother Dorothy's calm, even tones finished the Gloria.

Rising from her knees, Sister Joan felt, not a sudden blaze of illumination, but the unexcited certainty of knowledge. It had come into her mind during the very time when she wasn't thinking about it.

The full story wasn't yet clear but she knew who had killed Johnny Clare and Finn Boswell, Bryan and Serge and Patricia Mayne, and Sally too.

Mother Dorothy had given her permission to talk during the grand silence if she considered it necessary. Whether she would avail herself of the permission or not she didn't yet know, but she would certainly listen.

She left the chapel, the drops of water from the asperges still spotting her veil, and went through to the kitchen where Sister Teresa and Sister Marie were just going into the two lay cells that opened off it. They nodded, smilingly, in her direction, Sister Marie indicating Alice who, against all the rules, was tucked up in her basket instead of patrolling the grounds like the guard dog she was training to be.

She signalled to Sister Teresa to lock up behind her, unbolted the kitchen door, and stepped into the yard. The cobbles under her feet gleamed under the moon and as she stood still, accustoming her eyes to the darkness, the bulk of the stable, the outline of Lilith drowsing in her open stall, the scent of the fresh hay that had been piled within, the sounds of the wind as it rose and fell, scudding the wisps of dark cloud across the stars, became clear and immediate, real and familiar.

She had said she would be in the stable. Accordingly she entered and seated herself on the hay, her back against the wall, her skirt tucked modestly down, her hands folded.

There was a shadow thrown against the wall of the house by some trick of the light. A footfall sounded. Without moving, without raising her voice, she issued her invitation.

'You had better come in and tell me all about it.'

'You knew it was me?'

'Not with any certainty. Not until you said that Dodie would alibi her husband. I hadn't mentioned her husband. Nobody had.'

'But his tie-pin was left by the body.'

'And only Dodie and I knew that I'd found it. The only other person who knew was the one who put it there in the hope of incriminating him, not knowing that he was already dead.'

'Dead!' Derek took another step into the moonlight. 'What the devil are you talking about? Dodie's being questioned right now.'

'About his murder,' Sister Joan said.

'Dodie killed him? You're lying!'

'No, it's the truth,' Sister Joan said. 'She couldn't endure her ill-treatment any longer and she fears for her own children, so she killed him before she met you and Paul and travelled down here for the retreat. You knew Colin Mason, didn't you?'

'Since I killed the Clare boy,' Derek said. 'You know how it is. After we left college we all went our own ways and only ran into one another from time to time. I ran into Dodie and we had a cup of coffee together. She told me she was married, had children, painted pretty pictures for greetings cards. What she didn't know was that I knew her husband already. He and I, from time to time, frequented the same places. You know what I mean.'

'I can guess,' Sister Joan said with distaste.

'After that I contacted Colin again, mentioned I'd met his wife and that she was an old fellow-student of mine. I'd married Sally, of course. Nice girl Sally! Oh, in case you're wondering we had a perfectly satisfactory sex life. What is it they say? A woman for children, a boy for pleasure? Not that we ever managed to have children! Sally was disappointed about that. She compensated for it by taking over all my business affairs. At one time I was doing fairly well with portrait commissions, but then the recession came and we opened the fine arts shop. That just about kept our heads above water. I was very fond of Sally.'

'You didn't kill her?'

'I loved her!' he repeated, anger crackling in his voice. 'You're so damned narrow-minded you can't imagine that, can you? Sally was an integral part of my life! She didn't know about the – other. But she found out, I think. Yes, she found out.'

'That you'd killed Johnny Clare?'

'Colin Mason knew the Clares. That was a real stroke of luck. It led me straight to the boy. It was so simple. Colin helped me bury the body and after that, for safety's sake, we drifted apart.

And then the body was found six years later and the case was suddenly news again. Colin contacted me and we agreed to stay quiet. Always the best course of action. But Sally found out. Not everything but sufficient to make her worry, and the worry must have preyed on her mind because she went up to the top storey of that car-park, squeezed past the warning notice and jumped, fell, who knows?'

'Sally had asked Barbara to meet her,' Sister Joan said.

'Had she? I didn't know that. I knew they saw each other occasionally, of course. I knew that. Maybe she simply couldn't bring herself to talk to Barbara after all and decided to – telling someone that she thought I might have been involved in the murder of that boy wouldn't have changed what had happened.'

'That boy was Barbara's son,' Sister Joan said. 'Did you know that?'

'Of course I knew!' Derek took another pace forward. 'Bryan told me. He told me after Barbara told him about the child. He was pleased to think he'd sired a son. Bryan was pleased to think he'd sired a son! God, I never even guessed they'd ever slept together. He'd betrayed me with that mouse!'

'Betrayed you?' Sister Joan felt a long shiver run through her. 'Are you saying that you and Bryan – went to the same places?'

'Never!' Derek's handsome dark head went up. 'Bryan was a decent man. Fond of kids but forget anything else! In college we were – very close. Under age, of course, but we'd agreed that as soon as it was legally viable we'd live together. Discreetly, naturally. You didn't blazon those matters abroad in those days. But by the time we left college he'd gone off the idea. He went off by himself and lived alone, and I couldn't understand why. And then I met Serge and we got drunk together and Serge let it out. All the time Bryan was making promises to me he was sleeping with Barbara!'

'Once. It happened only once.'

'Once! Half a dozen times? Where's the difference? It was betrayal. Bryan threw me over for a stupid girl. He had a son! He had a son and Sally couldn't have children. I had to find the Clares, find Johnny, punish Bryan for his disloyalty. You see that?'

'I see that you would look upon it in that way,' Sister Joan said.

'Serge had known about it all along,' Derek was continuing. 'He knew and he said nothing, nothing! He knew who'd adopted the boy and he let that out too, so I had to find him. It took a long time. Months of checking, months of following and then I met up with Colin and he told me where the Clares lived, where Johnny went to school.'

'And Barbara and Bryan never guessed that you were the one who'd killed him?'

'They were old friends of mine,' Derek said. 'Barbara wasn't aware that Bryan had told me about the child. She didn't know that Bryan's first loyalty should have been to me. And Bryan never thought for a moment that his old college friend had anything to do with it at all. He told me once that he was glad our relationship was more normal. Normal! He talked a load of crap about our both having gone through a phase, as if we'd both suffered the measles! Sally and I were married and he thought a happy marriage proved all sorts of things. Stupid!'

'And then Barbara and Sally became friendly again.'

'I didn't know that Sally had asked Barbara to meet her. I didn't know,' Derek said. 'And I'm sure Sally never knew that Barbara had had a child. But something bothered her and, in the end, she stumbled into space and fell. My lovely, sensible, caring Sally! It was Bryan's fault, of course! If he hadn't betrayed me and sired a son then Johnny Clare wouldn't have been born, wouldn't have had to die.'

'So you killed Bryan,' Sister Joan said.

'He liked to take long country walks,' Derek said. 'Very early in the morning I waited and saw him, tramping along and whistling. He never knew what had hit him! I had a quick look through his pockets in case he had some money on him. Then the police could've thought it was a robbery. He had the photo we'd had taken, copies of it, all ready to send out to remind people of the reunion this year. I decided to send them out nearer the time. I even sent one to him, but I don't think it was ever opened or any notice taken of it. There are other people living in his cottage now.'

'You really wanted a reunion?' Sister Joan looked at him, at the handsome head silvered by moonlight, the proud stance.

'I enjoyed college,' he said simply. 'I thought it would be interesting to meet everybody again. I told Serge that.'

'You were seeing Serge?'

'Now and then, just as a mate. Serge only liked girls. The Platonic ideal escaped him.'

'Did it indeed?' Sister Joan said dryly. Her fear was ebbing and something akin to anger was replacing it.

Derek had killed a child out of spite. It was as clear as that. He had killed Johnny because Johnny was the son of the man he considered had betrayed him.

'I went round to see him one evening,' Derek said. 'You know that Sally and I had lived for a time when we were first married in the same apartment block? Serge moved in as we moved out, but we weren't close. Anyway he told me he'd been sent a copy of the photograph and had decided to go to it. He said more. He told me about Barbara having returned to this country because she wanted to keep track of her child, and he said that he was building up a dossier of dates when various things had occurred with a view to checking up, to finding out who'd killed Johnny Clare and Bryan. He felt there was a connection somewhere. He said that you'd been involved in a case down here, helping the police, and he thought that you might put your finger on some clue. Oh, Serge always rambled on when he was drunk. All about Paul suddenly deciding to act the queen in the hope of infiltrating the gay scene and learning something relevant! He was too keen on finding out the facts. I had some dope on me. I don't use it myself but sometimes one has to give a little present in the circles I move in. I simply emptied a nice little selection into his drink when he was in the toilet and left him. He was already dead I think.'

'And then came to the reunion as if nothing had happened.'

'I had to work out who knew what,' Derek said. 'I had to go along with the idea that Barbara and Dodie and Paul had cooked up, that somehow we could put our heads together and find out the truth. Without telling you, of course. You're a nun and nuns don't play private detective unless it's forced upon them. I was worried though, very worried when you went round to the flat. Serge had mentioned a new girlfriend, a girl called Patricia Mayne. I didn't know how much he'd told her. I didn't know if you'd bump into her at the flat and learn something or other. I decided that she would be much safer out of the way.'

'So you killed her,' Sister Joan said flatly.

'After the theatre when we went our separate ways. I went to the flat, saw her coming out, introduced myself as an old friend of Serge's, walked up the road with her, paused by the betting shop, took a step back – it was over in a moment. Then I went back to the flat; the lock on the door was broken so no difficulty there, had a good look round and saw nothing. Maybe Serge hadn't any dossier at all. Maybe it had all been in his own head. But the rest of them weren't stupid. Sooner or later someone might start making connections and that might lead to me. Then I decided that it would be best if another child was killed and Colin Mason took the blame. He'd known the Clares and if he was linked to one murder he could easily be linked to the others. He'd lent me a tie-pin once. Rather a vulgar thing, but I'd worn it once or twice, so I brought it down with me.'

'And killed Finn Boswell,' Sister Joan said.

'Yes, that was the name.' Derek sounded indifferent. 'I slipped out while we were all milling around after we arrived, saw the kid playing and told him the sisters wanted to see him. We were just walking off when some crazy loon turned up. I pulled up my scarf, saying that I'd toothache, and the kid did my work for me, even called me Colin. I killed him straight off, hid him under some branches, dropped the tie-pin, and came back to help the little nun pick apples. It was so easy.'

'And then he was missing and the men from the camp came looking for him.'

'They would've found him sooner,' Derek said, 'but the loony—'

'Don't call him that!' Her anger bubbled forth. 'Luther is slow-witted, but not crazy. He's an innocent!'

'As you say. Anyway it wasn't up to me to find the body, so we came back to the postulancy. That's all really. I've been waiting all day for someone to connect the tie-pin with Colin Mason. And then you said Dodie had gone with the police—'

'Accused of murder.'

'I spoke too soon,' he said with charming regret. 'I assumed that Colin had been picked up and the police wanted to ask Dodie questions about him. That was a very careless thing for me to do.'

'So you've come back.' She rose slowly, standing with her

back against the wall.

'I made an excuse to Fiona and Barbara, nipped out of the pub and drove here. You did say you'd be in the stable.'

'And now you're going to kill me too?' Her hands were cold and she held them clasped tightly within the sleeves of her habit. 'What good will that do? You can't put the blame on Colin Mason. You can't stop the others from finding out the truth. Not now. The police know that Serge was working things out in his own mind – he left dates scribbled on a pile of old newspapers that contained accounts of Johnny Clare's killing and the finding of his remains. It's too late now.'

'Quite right, Sister!'

The two men who had just emerged from the stall where Lilith drowsed were, she decided, the most welcome people she'd ever seen.

'The police were here already?' Derek laughed, a sound horrifying in its casualness.

'I didn't know they were,' Sister Joan said.

'Miss Ford and Miss Madox came to the police station to see if they could help Mrs Mason,' Detective Sergeant Mill said, nodding to Constable Petrie. 'We drove up here, and concealed ourselves while you were in the chapel. Miss Ford said you'd announced that you'd be in the stable, so it seemed the logical place to wait. Mr Derek Smith, you're under arrest for murder—'

'It was a necessary punishment,' Derek said. 'Bryan was unfaithful to the promise we'd made to live together. He and Barbara had had a child. They'd had a child that Barbara gave away and my Sally couldn't have children. My Sally started suspecting something was wrong and Serge talked to her; Serge put suspicion in her mind, so she didn't want to go on living. She fretted and fretted and in the end she didn't meet Barbara at all. And the others were getting together for the reunion, starting to piece things together. I wasn't going to kill you, Joan. Why bother? You haven't been disloyal.'

'Be with you in a moment,' Detective Sergeant Mill said.

She nodded, turning to where Lilith stood, snorting slightly as the voices and the movement roused her from her doze, Lilith's coat felt rough and warm and safe.

The sound of a car starting up was followed by footsteps in the cobbled yard.

'Are you all right, Sister?' Detective Sergeant Mill asked.

'I think so.' She turned, her hand still stroking Lilith's nose.

'He's mentally sick of course.'

'Yes, that's what they'll say, isn't it? Evil has no place in the modern world.'

'I'm merely a policeman,' he said.

'You knew it was Derek?'

'Your friend Dodie knew that her husband and Derek Smith met occasionally. She'd blotted out the fact that they probably enjoyed the same – shall we say pleasures? – but when she saw the tie-pin she knew that her husband was already dead and couldn't have had anything to do with Finn Boswell's death.'

'Perhaps deep down they were all beginning to know,' Sister Joan said. 'Paul said he'd lost his driving licence and came down with Derek and Dodie in Derek's car. I wonder if he felt uneasy about their being alone together without quite knowing why. And Dodie insisted on going with Barbara and Derek when they went for a walk. Somewhere in her mind she must have felt uneasy about him.'

'Mrs Mason will get bail and, I'm certain, after all the facts are known, a suspended sentence,' the detective sergeant said.

'I hope so. It's all such a tangle!' She pushed a straying curl of black hair back beneath her veil. 'Everyone had a little piece of the puzzle. Even Fiona had been a teacher at Johnny Clare's school and Serena must've sensed that Paul was heterosexual all along.'

'We expect to get a lot of help from the gay community on this,' he said. 'Contrary to what you might think most of them are very much against child molesters.'

'I never thought anything of the sort!' she said indignantly. 'Alan, if Bryan had kept his promise and made his life with Derek maybe none of this would've happened. Promises are so important! A broken promise is a breach of fidelity and when that is breached then there's no truth or trust left.'

'It's getting late.' He put out his hand, briefly touching her arm. 'You've been very brave and rather foolish, as usual. With your written statement about this last interview and Derek Smith's own state of mind the case will be cut and dried. No need for you to be involved further.'

'He really loved Sally, you know.' She spoke soberly and

sadly as they left the stable together. 'He really did depend on her. After Sally died he went after Bryan, and then after Serge and then poor Patricia Mayne, and then – all because of a broken promise!'

'I'll have a few words with the others and then get back to the station to complete the formalities. Are you coming?'

'You talk to them. I've taken advantage of Mother Dorothy's leave to speak for long enough.'

'Sister, you ought to talk to somebody,' he said. 'You've just been on an emotional rollercoaster, not knowing what to believe about people who were once your friends, not knowing whom to trust. Even nuns require a bit of counselling now and then.'

'Don't worry, Alan.' She gave him a teasing, kindly glance. 'I have good counsel already, a friend who always listens. Good night.'

Turning, she walked briskly down the side of the great house, heading for the outer door which gave access to the chapel at every hour. There would be good counsel there, she thought, and no broken promises. Nothing but the silence that calmed the heart.

Later she would talk to the others, do what she could to help Dodie, but for the moment she must go where her first fidelity was housed.